7/31

JUST JEALOUS

D0257620

ANNE CASSIDY

JUST JEALOUS

worse
people be
d, 1,000 are se
ps rescued 300
ple from rubble
y could hear mo
n the debris bu
them out becau

ngerprint

POLICE have launched
a murder hunt after
discovering the body
of a teenaged boy in a
park yesterday in
Colby East. The seven-
teen-year-old boy ap-
pears to have been
killed by a single gun-
shot wound to the
chest though police
would not confirm de-
tails at press time.
immediate arrests, but
are investigating
crime and are ap-
ing to the public
any potential wit-
es. The victim has
et been formally

BY E

police
At thi
lieve
not i
terca
he w
tance
tem
cause
have
bou
cont
it m
police
the cr
pealin
for an

■SCHOLASTIC

First published in the UK in 2009 by Scholastic Children's Books
An imprint of Scholastic Ltd
Euston House, 24 Eversholt Street
London, NW1 1DB, UK
Registered office: Westfield Road, Southam, Warwickshire, CV47 0RA
SCHOLASTIC and associated logos are trademarks and/or
registered trademarks of Scholastic Inc.

ISBN 978 1407 104041

A CIP catalogue record for this book
is available from the British Library.

Printed and bound in Great Britain by CPI Bookmarque, Croydon
Papers used by Scholastic Children's Books are made from wood grown in
sustainable forests.

1 3 5 7 9 10 8 6 4 2

www.scholastic.co.uk/zone

O, beware, my lord, of jealousy;
It is the green-ey'd monster. . .

Othello, William Shakespeare

PART ONE

PART ONE

ONE

New Year's Day

It was as if Elise wasn't there. No one could hear her. No one could see her. She wasn't visible. She stood behind the tree and looked across the grass at the tiny play area. Daylight was just breaking, raw and unfriendly. The sky was the colour of a wet dishcloth. The air was full of rain prickling at her face. She could taste salt from the sea. She wiped her fingers across her skin, licking her lips like a dog.

Peter Fenner was there, lying face down on the tarmac, as if he were in a deep sleep. His leather coat covered him like a tarpaulin; only his boots were sticking out. Elise closed her eyes tightly for a few seconds, to block it out, to steady herself, to stave off the panic that was gripping her insides.

The grass in the field was swaying in the wind like liquid. The swings were listing, floating towards her and away. The metal horse on springs shivered. There was movement everywhere and yet everything was still. It made her head feel light so she held on tightly to the tree, her nails digging into the bark.

At the corner of her eye the light became intense. She

turned and saw a bulb of blue flashing excitably on top of a car just outside the park. She held her breath and clung to the tree. It wouldn't be long before everyone knew. She sucked air in as the car nosed through the gate and came forward slowly, its wheels hardly turning. Then it stopped.

Nothing happened.

Elise leaned out from behind the tree, her face wet now but her mouth as dry as stone. She couldn't see into the car but she imagined they were sitting working out what to do. A boy passed out in Marsh Park. A leftover from New Year's Eve. It was early in the morning and they'd jump to conclusions: *Just another teenager getting up to no good. Drugs or drink.* They would be worried about exposure. The North Sea wind was arctic at times. They'd be calling for an ambulance. Maybe it was leaving at that very moment, its doors slamming, its engine revving, its siren waking suddenly like an alarm clock.

The driver's door opened and a uniformed officer got out. He shook his legs as if he were stiff, doing up the zip of his jacket and raising his collar against the cold. A gust of wind rolled over him on to the grass, making waves on the surface. It broke as it hit the trees, sending icy air up her sleeves, in her collar, drenching her face. She felt herself tremble.

Then he walked towards the body.

She pushed her forehead into the rough bark. She closed her eyes. Inside her head she saw Carl's shocked face the previous evening. Carl, the boy she loved. She should have known that he would do something. That it would end badly. She knew everything else, after all. She was everywhere. She was invisible.

She heard a shout and running feet. The policeman had seen the blood on Peter's coat, dark red, almost maroon against the black leather. She watched as he ran back to the car and spoke rapidly through the driver's window. The passenger door was flung open and the other officer got out. He was stern-faced, and as he walked, he seemed to be looking at the ground, his eyes darting about here and there. When he got to the body he stood very still and rubbed his forehead with his hand. He said something. The same word over and over. She could see by the shape of his mouth that he was swearing. Then he dropped down on to his knees, his head bent, concentrating. For a bizarre moment she thought he was praying, but then she realized that he was searching for something.

The weapon.

Elise's jaw froze. She hadn't done that. Why not? Why hadn't she? She could have looked for it. She'd spent all that time standing there staring at the body when she could have found the gun; maybe it would have been on the ground, in the grass, by the swings, in the bushes. She could have picked up Andy's gun and hidden it away but now it was too late.

In the distance she heard what sounded like a siren. She shrank away. With one last look at the body lying on the ground she slipped back into the trees, where there was no possibility of anyone seeing her.

Then she ran away.

PART TWO

TWO

October

Carl Murdoch wouldn't let her down. Elise knew that.

She stared into the mirror above the row of washbasins. Her hair looked odd, longer one side than the other. Maybe it would be better up top. She pulled it up with her hands, scrutinized it for a moment, and then let it drop. She reached into her jacket pocket and pulled out a plum lip liner. She went close to the mirror and painted it on. Stepping back, she pursed her lips and looked at herself. It was too obvious, and anyway, Carl didn't like make-up. She turned back into one of the cubicles and pulled off a line of toilet paper. She wiped the lipstick off.

She took her mobile out of her other pocket and looked reproachfully at it. It was 13.47. There was no ring tone, no beep, no message, no explanation about why he hadn't arrived. He knew that the hearing started at two. She'd called him and confirmed it the previous night. *I'll be there, no worry*, he'd said.

Outside the court building she joined her mum and her brother, Andy. Everywhere she looked there were small groups of people looking anxious.

The three of them were formally dressed. Andy was in

a suit and dark tie, his shoes polished as though he were on the parade ground. Her mum was in a navy skirt suit, her long hair pulled up in a pleat. Elise was wearing black trousers and jacket with a white fitted shirt. The three of them looked like they were guests at a wedding, not people waiting for a judgement. Her brother, puffing on a cigarette, smiling at something her mum had said, didn't look like someone who was about to hear how long he had to spend in prison.

Where was Carl? Elise looked past people to the street beyond. There was no sign of him.

"Maybe they'll give you Community?" her mum said.

Elise bristled with impatience. How many times were they going to have this conversation? She watched her brother suck on his cigarette. He didn't lift his eyes off the ground. It was up to her to answer her mum.

"He'll go to prison, Mum. That's what the solicitor said. It was a violent assault."

"But the man's all right, isn't he? He's not got any lasting damage?"

"There's CCTV footage of Andy kicking him when he was on the ground."

"He wasn't the only one," her mum said.

Elise narrowed her eyes. "He was the only one who turned round and faced the camera."

"Cheer me up, why don't you?" Andy said, brushing the front of his suit down.

Elise turned to her brother. He was only twenty-five but he looked ten years older. He was tall and muscular, his army training giving him broad shoulders and a thick neck. In his suit he was like a bouncer standing outside a nightclub. His face had broadened. He'd gone into the army a good-looking young man. Five years later he looked bloated, as if his features had shrunk back into his head. Sometimes it made her feel as if she hardly knew him.

"But they'll take the war into account. They'll see that," her mum said.

Elise shrugged. Andy had been back from Iraq for over a year. She wondered if the judge would take any notice.

"Hey, don't worry about me," Andy said, lighting up another cigarette. "I've done the crime, I'll do the time!"

Elise didn't say anything. Andy didn't seem worried about the idea of prison. Elise had tried several times to talk to him about it but he'd dismissed it, spending most of his time in the garage working on his jeep. Even Carl had sounded him out. A couple of times he'd gone into the garage and helped Andy rub at the paintwork or dismantle bits of the engine. *He just doesn't seem bothered*, Carl had said when she asked him afterwards. He could have been hiding his feelings. She just couldn't work him out, not since he'd left the army.

"We ought to go in," she said, her eyes scanning the street, looking to see if Carl was running up, out of breath, full of apologies.

"Let me finish this ciggy," Andy said.

"I need to go to the toilet, anyway," her mum said.

Elise watched her mum go into the court buildings.

The suit she was wearing was too tight and too short, especially with the low-heeled boots. It made her look like a dark square on top of fat legs. If only she'd worn the trousers that Elise had suggested.

"Don't forget, if you get any enquiries about car ads, just give them Johnson's number," Andy said. "The only motor I've got is the jeep and that's not part of the business. Johnson knows that."

She nodded. He'd given her all these instructions the previous night. Since leaving the army, he and a mate had been buying and selling cars for a living. The jeep was something he'd found at a crash auction and he was doing it up for himself.

"Three months is all I'll get," Andy said. "I'll be out in eight weeks with good behaviour. Might be able to finish the jeep in time for Christmas. Maybe put it on eBay."

"You shouldn't be so confident," she said. "It's like tempting fate."

"Oh, Elly. Lighten up," he said, posting his dog-end into the air. "You always expect the worst thing to happen. Look at me, I'm a lucky boy. I went to Iraq and came back without a scratch. I'll get three months in some open nick and I'll be back in time to help you put the Christmas decorations up."

Exasperated, she turned away – and there, coming towards her, was Carl. She felt her throat tighten when she saw him. She did her jacket up and smoothed it down. Then she undid it again and made sure the buttons on her blouse were fastened.

"All right, Andy?" Carl said, holding out his hand.

Andy shook his hand. It was something that amused Elise. They saw each other almost every day, yet away from the street it was always a handshake, as though they hadn't met for months.

"Hey, sorry I'm late. This job that my dad was on took for ever. We were waiting for a delivery of timber. Anyway. . ." Carl said, holding his hands out.

She shrugged her shoulders. She was just pleased to see him. He stood directly in front of her. He had dressed up, dark trousers and a zip-up jacket and shoes, not trainers. She wanted to put her hand out and touch his arm but suddenly felt shy. They were friends. Sometimes they hugged but it was always without thought, on the spur of the moment. Sometimes they kissed like boyfriend and girlfriend but it was nearly always in the dark, when there was alcohol or dope around.

"Here's the spare garage key," Andy said, pulling a key ring out of his pocket.

It hung in the air for a moment, a leather fob with a single Chubb key. Carl took it.

"There's a lot of rust on the jeep. It's weeks of work. You do it for me and I'll see you all right when I come out."

"Is it certain you'll get Custodial?" Carl said, pocketing the key.

Andy nodded.

"Here's Mum," Elise said.

Her mum was coming towards them, half running, looking as though something important had happened.

"Hi, Carl!" she said and then, grabbing Andy's sleeve, "I've just seen Mr Joseph. He says we ought to go in. He wants a last-minute word."

"Right," Andy said. "Let's get this over with."

He walked off in the direction of the doors. Elise watched him, his big shoulders sloping down, his hands patting at the sides of his jacket, the trousers of his suit flapping. A feeling of trepidation gripped her. All his bravado would count for nothing when he was locked up. She'd felt the same when he joined the army. He'd been like a puppy dog then, showing off his uniform, his eyes glittering with excitement, constantly talking about what training was going to be like, what sort of career soldier he was going to be. All she'd kept thinking about was him getting hurt or maybe hurting someone else. Now he'd done it anyway. On a Saturday night in Norwich.

"Andy, wait," she shouted.

She quickened her step to catch up with him. He paused and looked round. For a second he looked puzzled, and then his face broke into a smile. Elise put her arms out and gave him an awkward hug.

"Oh, Andy," she said, her face against his jacket, "will you be all right?"

"Hey, sis," he said, his big arm grasping her shoulder, "don't worry about your big brother. I know how to look after myself."

He let her go and walked on, through the swing doors, heading for her mum and Mr Joseph.

"He'll be OK, Elly," Carl said, his hand on her arm as

they followed him into the building. "His solicitor says he'll get three months. He was a soldier. That'll go well for him."

She nodded. Things sounded better when Carl said them. Maybe they were all right. She should stop looking on the dark side of life. Be optimistic. Andy would get prison, but he would be out well before Christmas.

THREE

The cafeteria had a low ceiling and no windows. It was probably her imagination but she felt, for a few moments, as if there wasn't enough air in there to breathe. It was crowded and there was a lot of talk that seemed unbearably loud after the quiet of the courtroom. Elise blew her nose into a bunch of tissues. Her eyes felt dry and gritty but at least she'd stopped crying. Carl was up at the counter getting some drinks.

Andy had been given a twelve-month prison sentence.

She'd gasped when it had been read out. Even Andy had looked shaken. Then he'd turned to her and her mum and given a tiny mock salute before the policeman led him away. As if he didn't care.

Carl came back to the table carrying two paper cups of tea.

"I didn't get one for your mum because I didn't know how long it would take her to see the solicitor."

Elise nodded. She pictured her mum crying on Mr Joseph's shoulder. Twelve months! It was harsh. It seemed as though the fact that Andy had been in the army had made it worse for him, not better. The judge had virtually sneered when he gave the sentence. *Members of the armed forces have an even bigger responsibility when they return home from active duty. Andrew Hanson, you have been trained to protect and defend. You do not have the right to use that training when you are out on a drunken night in Norwich.*

Elise picked up the cup to drink from it but felt her hand trembling, so she put it back down again.

"How will he manage? For a whole year?" she said.

"It won't be that long. He'll get parole. He might even get early release. You hear about these things."

"What things?" she said, looking straight at Carl.

"Overcrowding in prison. Sometimes they release people early."

"Do they?" she said.

He nodded.

"But a whole year. . ."

"It won't be a year. If he keeps his nose clean, he'll be out next spring." Carl blew on his tea and gulped it down. "Come on, you know what Andy's like. He'll be buying and selling stuff in there!"

"Prison memorabilia?" she said, managing a half smile.

"Absolutely. He'll put it on eBay when he gets out."

"EBay!"

Carl was grinning. That was Andy's answer to everything. *Put it on eBay.*

She drank her tea and gazed around the packed cafeteria. Somewhere, in another part of the building, her brother was sitting waiting to be taken to prison. What would he be travelling in? A white van with slits for windows. Inside it men would sit in cubicles, their families and friends already somewhere in the past, a kind of half life ahead of them.

The exit doors opened to let people out and Elise saw her mum edging through. She dragged a nearby chair over and Carl stood up and pulled out some coins from his pocket.

"Get Mum a milky tea?" she said.

He nodded, picked up his own drink and moved away just as her mum sat down.

"Mr Joseph says that Andy might be able to appeal the sentence," she said, breathlessly. "He's going to look into it. He says the judge was completely wrong not to take his Iraq posting into consideration!"

Elise nodded.

"If Andy had been on the ground then he would have been the one who got kicked. It's what men do. Fight. Wasn't that what he was sent to Iraq to do? Fight?"

"It's not quite the same, Mum."

"Mr Joseph says Andy may well be suffering from some kind of post-trauma thingy."

"Post-traumatic stress syndrome," Elise said.

"That's it! He's going to look into it."

Carl came back and placed her mum's drink on the table.

"I think I'll take this outside, make a call," her mum said.

She picked up the drink and pulled her mobile out of her jacket pocket. Elise watched her go out of the doors.

Her walk had a spring in it. She really thought there might be a chance to get Andy out.

"She thinks that there'll be an appeal," she said.

"If it makes her feel better."

"But if it raises Andy's hopes and then it doesn't happen?"

"It'll get them over the first couple of months. It'll give Andy something to do, prepare his case, read his papers. Then it'll be Christmas. And who knows? Maybe the appeal will work. It'll make the time seem shorter either way."

"What about me? It won't seem shorter for me."

"With all the *exciting* stuff you've got to look forward to? Helping me strip out the Beachcomber? The trip to Norwich to see the play? Then, don't forget, best of all, there's your chance to become a star in the school Christmas concert. You know how much you look forward to that."

She shook her head, her face softening. Inside she felt a bit lighter, as if things might not be as bad as she thought. Carl was right. Maybe an appeal would be a good thing. It might get Andy and Mum through the first few months. She finished her tea and sat back.

"Anyway, I know what will cheer you up," Carl said.

"What?" She had a quizzical look on her face.

Carl put his hand in his pocket. "It cost me a lot of money."

She smiled. She knew what was coming. He held out a tube of sweets.

"Here; don't say I never buy you anything."

Wine gums. It was months since she'd had those.

"My favourite. Thanks. And thanks for coming. I really appreciate it."

"I said I'd stay over at Dad's tonight but I really should come home with you two. You shouldn't be on your own," he said.

"No," Elise said, "we'll be all right. We'll jump on the bus and be home in no time. Probably get a takeaway."

"You sure?"

"We'll be OK. Not so sure about Andy, though."

"He's tough. He managed in Iraq. He'll be all right."

She nodded her head. Inside, though, she wasn't so sure.

FOUR

Their bus was sitting at its port. Its lights were on and its doors were open. On the front the digital display moved gently past, listing the route home. *Norwich East: Wroxham: Lessingham: Walcott: Colby East.* Elise stepped into it and felt warm air on her legs and face. Her shoulders softened and her arms loosened. She hadn't realized how stiff she'd been. She and her mum showed their passes and went up to the back. It would be a long ride, forty minutes or more. Her mum sat next to the window and she was on the aisle. There were other passengers, sitting in ones and twos, looking tired, their faces ruddy from the cold outside or the heat of the bus.

She looked out of the window at the brightly lit garage. It was huge, its big curved roof like a sports stadium. There were people milling about, heading for different buses. For a second it felt like any other day, as if she'd been shopping and was going home laden with purchases, keen for the bus to move off and head for the coast road so that she could get home, slip next door and show Carl the things she'd bought. It wasn't any other day, though. Her brother was in prison.

The bus started. Elise felt it vibrate underneath her as it

moved in a slow circle around the perimeter of the bus station. Then it pushed out on to the road. She looked past her mum, through the glass, her eyes darting here and there at the surrounding traffic. She had an idea that they might pass the security van that was taking Andy away. It was unlikely but she sat forward, willing it to appear, to come alongside them. If only she could just see it. It would be like two ships slicing through the water, setting out on different journeys.

But she didn't see the van and eventually sat back.

The bus moved briskly along and they sank into silence. They headed away from the shops and brightness of town. They passed through the housing estates, stopping to pick up passengers. Out of Norwich the bus went on to a dual carriageway and sat in the inside lane, cars and lorries thundering past it. Beyond the road she could see swathes of darkness as the bus headed out towards the coast. After the dual carriageway it was blacker, the bus moving along a single-lane country road, regularly overtaken by cars. There were a few stops where passengers got off but no one else got on, and the bus emptied itself at Walcott, the last town before Colby East. Elise got her mobile and looked at the time. It was five thirty. She had a whole evening ahead of her alone with her mum. The thought weighed heavily on her. At some point Mum would start to worry about telling people; friends and neighbours and the other staff at Palmer's where she worked. And Gran hadn't been mentioned yet, which was a relief.

Since Gran died, almost a year before, everything that happened to them was considered from her point of view. At Christmas and at birthdays it was the good things – presents, meals and family pleasures. At some stage her mum would stand amid it all and say, *If only Gran could see this.* At times of trouble, when the money was low, when Mum's health was bad, when Andy left the army, it was, *I'm glad your gran's not here to see this.* Gran, her mum's mum, whose house they'd lived in ever since her father left them, had been a big presence in their lives. Elise had only been three months old when they moved in, so memories of her childhood were full of her gran.

Even though she was dead, their house was still cluttered with her personal possessions. Some of Gran's clothes still hung in her mum's wardrobe; photographs of her at various ages were on the walls, dotted across the house; her special china was still used for important family meals. Elise even had some of Gran's theatrical stuff: feathers and paste jewellery that she'd used to dress up in when she was much younger. Reminders of Gran were everywhere.

Up ahead were the lights of her school, which was just outside of the town. The whole building was illuminated, the bright yellow classrooms throwing out a glow over the black countryside. They sped past, coming up to the sign that said *Welcome to Colby East.* The outskirts of the town looked dark and closed up. *As usual*, Elise thought. After six o'clock, out of season, what was there to do in Colby East? Two pubs, a Chinese takeaway, an off-licence and a minicab office. Everywhere else was shut. The next town was four miles along the coast road.

The bus swung into the high street, passing the handful of shops that made up the town. Most of them were closed. The only one still open was Palmer's. *What a dump*, Elise thought. Colby East twinned with nowhere. Eleven-hundred-plus people living in a village clinging to the Norfolk coast, row after row of houses huddled against the North Sea air. In the summer it made for a fresh breeze but in the winter the cold took your breath away, sinking into your pores like ice water.

"Mr Palmer will be wanting to know about Andy," her mum said.

"You don't have to tell him *tonight*."

They were heading for the bus turning-circle. When it stopped they got off. Elise stepped out of the bus first and felt the cold air slicing into her skin. Her mum made a loud shivering noise. They bent their heads down and walked into the fierce wind that was coming in waves off the sea.

"Shall we get a takeaway?" Elise said, seeing the Chinese up ahead.

Her mum shook her head. Elise could tell, by the way her mouth was tightly closed, that she was holding back the tears. Elise put her arm around her and gave her a hug.

"We'll get through this," she said. "Look on the bright side. At least he's not still in Iraq."

Her mum nodded "The appeal might work, mightn't it, Elly?"

"It might," Elise said.

They quickened up, turning into their street, her mum fiddling with her bag to get her keys out. Pulling the front door open, they were hit by the heat.

"Lovely and warm!" her mum said.

"Like a sauna, you mean," Elise said.

Her mum turned the lights on and walked ahead of her into the living room. She stopped in the middle and looked above the mantlepiece. There were photos of her gran there from many years before. The largest showed a beautiful young woman in dancing clothes staring out at them. Elise tensed. She knew what was coming.

"Oh, Elly, what would your gran think? Andy in prison like a common criminal. What would she say?"

Elise didn't answer. She sat down on the sofa, fanning herself to keep cool.

FIVE

It wasn't an accident that Elise saw Carl being dropped off by his dad the next afternoon. She'd been waiting for his return from Norwich. When the car pulled up just after three she was standing at her mum's bedroom window looking out on to the street. It only took a second to go downstairs, grab her leather jacket and open the front door. She strode out as if she had somewhere to go. Carl and his dad were on the pathway coming in her direction. She looked surprised to see them.

"Everything OK?" Carl said.

"Fine," Elise said.

Carl's dad, Michael, gave a sympathetic look.

"Sorry to hear about your brother," he said.

Michael was a nice man. He'd lived next door to her until a couple of years before, when he'd left to go and live with a woman in Norwich. She listened for a moment as he went on to say how much he'd liked Andy, and talked about how he'd fixed his car for him on several occasions over the years. She nodded politely and saw then, as she had done in the past, the striking resemblance between Carl and his dad. Both of them were tall and thin. Both had big smiles and slightly crooked teeth. Both had brown eyes. Michael's skin was much darker than Carl's but anyone would have known immediately that they were related. Carl was light brown, his skin the colour of polished wood.

Carl's front door opened and his mum, Penny, stood there.

"You said you'd have him back for school!" she said.

There was a change in the atmosphere. Michael stiffened and Carl became awkward, stepping forward and back as if he didn't know whether he wanted to go in or stay with his dad. Elise couldn't find any reason to stand there, so she walked off down the path as the voices behind her rose and then there was the sound of the front door banging. She looked back. They had all gone inside.

There was always trouble when Michael turned up. Carl had told her that his parents disagreed about everything to do with him and that there were constant rows; face to face, by telephone or even by letter.

She headed on down the street. Maybe it would be easier for Carl if he had no contact at all with his dad, like her and Andy. It had made life simpler for them. They hadn't had any squabbles over who was having who at weekends. There had never been rows over money, or parents trying to agree which schools they went to. Life had been easier with just one parent.

She found herself at the sea wall, aimless. She leaned on the railings and watched as the waves lazily lapped at the shore, the rim of the water lacy as it broke over layers of pebbles. When the water receded the sand was hard-packed and almost brown. She looked further along at the huge concrete blocks that had been added to the beach to stop coastal erosion. They lay at angles like giant dice that had been carelessly tossed into the air. Further on, out of sight, the sand was wider, softer, easy prey for the North Sea wind that blew it inland and formed the dunes. In summer, on a good day, it was packed with people. In October it was deserted.

It wasn't as cold as it had been the day before. Elise looked along at the Beachcomber Café, which sat back from the sea wall. She and Carl had spent time there in recent weeks. He'd worked there on and off through the summer. The owner, who Carl's mum worked for, had given him the keys and asked him to clear the place, to clean and decorate it ready for next year. He was getting cash in hand every couple of weeks for what he'd done. A week before she'd helped him clear out the old larder. It had been fun. The place was boarded up so no one could see in. They'd had the heater on and some music from an old CD player that Carl kept there. She'd brought a bottle of wine from her mum's cupboard and poured it into polystyrene cups as soon as she got there. It wasn't a big space, just the size of a mobile home, so they kept elbowing each other or stepping on each other's feet. They had to work as a team and they talked and joked as Carl pulled giant tins of baked beans from shelves at the back, some of them past their sell-by date by a year or more. Squatting down to pull out some old pots and pans, she'd felt a rush of movement and squealed as a number of mice scooted across the floor under her legs, disappearing in moments down cracks in the floor.

Carl had pulled her up. *It's only a few mice*, he'd laughed, but she'd been screaming, going totally over the top, and he'd put his arms around her to calm her down.

And then they were kissing. She had no idea who started it but he was close and she felt his arms around her, the heat of his chest against hers, and they'd ended up mouth to mouth, him moving her backwards so that they were leaning up against the wall of the larder. Elise had let herself flop in his arms, her body like jelly up against the wall, her chest tingling, her legs falling open as he leant into her, his tongue in her mouth.

She'd thought she would swoon with pleasure.

She stared at the sea, warmed by the memory. The waves were breaking further out, the sky charcoal. Maybe there would be rain or a storm. She thought of Andy, spending his first day in prison. He would be looking at four walls. It gave her a dragging feeling in her chest. He'd said it didn't matter to him. *I've done the crime, I'll do the time*, he'd said. Had he meant it? How could she tell? Andy kept everything close to his chest, like when she asked him about Iraq. *Piece of cake*, he'd said, but she knew it hadn't been as easy as that.

A sound distracted her. It was a ring tone that sounded like a car screeching to a halt. Loads of the kids in school had them. It set her teeth on edge and she looked round to see a familiar face walking along the sea wall in her direction. It was Jason Bell from her form. He was talking on his mobile and he gestured to her. The call finished quickly and then he was standing beside her.

"Heard about your brother. Bad luck," he said.

"Um," she said.

A sharp beep came from his mobile.

"Text," he said, explaining.

As if she didn't know. She rolled her eyes while he read over his text. She didn't dislike Jason Bell but he was a bit dopey. And in any case he wasn't the person she wanted to be with.

"Todd said he should have slipped the police a few quid. Todd knows a couple of bent coppers. He should have asked him," Jason said, looking up from his mobile.

Elise didn't answer. Todd Bell, Jason's older brother, had once been a mate of Andy's. After his short spell in prison a couple of years before, Todd liked to boast about his life of crime. He hung around the younger kids hinting that he could get stuff for people; iPods, mobiles, any kind of drug. Apart from an occasional lump of dope, Elise had never seen any of it. Todd's real job was as a minicab driver, using his flashy BMW to ferry people back and forth to school or the supermarket.

"Fancy a walk?" he said. "Over by the sand dunes?"

She looked at him with exasperation. He was talking in a code. The sand dunes meant a snog. At least in June or July it did. In October it meant hypothermia.

"I can't; I'm seeing someone."

"Carl Murdoch?" he said.

"No! Not *Carl*. I'm meeting someone. In a while," she said, looking at her watch.

"I got the keys to the BMW. You could wait there. It'll be warm?"

Jason's mobile beeped again.

"Text," he said.

She frowned. It had just gone four and she had the rest of the day to fill. There was every possibility that Carl wouldn't come out at all. She looked at Jason. He was using his thumb to text, his eyes riveted to his mobile, his shoulders bent over, the tip of his tongue showing at his mouth as if he was doing something really skilled like brain surgery. She certainly didn't fancy Jason but it was still only late afternoon and there was an ocean of time to fill.

"I'd like to hear about Andy," he said, without looking up. "Todd will want to know."

She turned and looked back towards the town. The place was deserted except for a few of the younger kids from school sitting on the sea wall. She could always just go home. But then she might run into Carl or his dad and it would look funny, as though she'd not really had anywhere to go in the first place.

"Come on then," she said, "I'll wait in the car."

Jason stopped texting, an expression of surprise on his face, as if he hadn't expected her to agree.

"It's in the beach car park," he said.

She turned her back on the sea and began to walk in the direction of the dunes. He was beside her in an instant. They went past the Beachcomber and along to the end of the sea wall. Then she stepped off the concrete walkway on to a track and headed towards the sand dunes. They took a well-worn path that wound its way through the dunes until they came out on the other side and stepped into the beach car park. It was small, room for about twenty cars, and in the summer it was often full. Now it was almost empty.

The BMW was in the far corner.

Jason pressed the remote and the side lights flicked on and off and she heard the clunk of the doors unlocking. He quickened his step, moving ahead of her, and opened the back door. He waited for her as she walked the last few paces across the car park. She couldn't help but look around the dusky space, the dunes on one side, the houses of the town on the other. In between, the car park had a misty look, as though the concrete ground was attracting thicker air. It seemed warmer, the cold trapped on the other side of the sand dunes.

"You coming?" Jason said, getting into the car.

Why not? She walked around to the other door, got in and made herself comfortable.

"Which nick is Andy in?" he said.

She was about to answer when Jason ducked down and began rummaging under the seat for something. A moment later he came up with a small bottle of spirits. Vodka.

"Which nick, did you say?" he said, and then, holding

the bottle towards her, he added, "Want some? I mixed it with lemonade."

She reached out and took the bottle, unscrewing the top. She took a gulp and felt the bubbles on her throat. Behind the sweetness of the lemonade was something else, harder, hotter. She took a second gulp and then handed it back to Jason. He didn't drink it; he just put the bottle down and leaned across her, his fingers playing with the zip of her jacket.

"You could undo this. It's warm enough," he said, his voice husky.

"Andy's prison is in Essex," she said, pulling the zip down until her jacket fell open.

"Essex," he said, looking down at her chest.

A second later he was kissing her, his lips just touching hers, tentative, nervous. She held back for a moment but then felt herself responding, closing her eyes, pulling at his arm to draw him closer. After some long kisses his hand fluttered across her breast and his mouth dropped down to her neck and brushed against her skin.

She let herself sink back into the seat. Opening her eyes she saw that the interior of the car was dusky, almost like night-time. It made her feel sleepy.

A noise startled her. Three sharp taps on the glass. She sat up quickly and pulled her clothes together. She moved a few centimetres away from Jason as if to distance herself from him. There, at the window was the round, boyish face of Todd Bell. He was grinning in a disgusting way. Jason pressed the button and the window slid down.

"What's up?" he said.

"I need the motor. Got some important business to do," Todd said.

"You mean you've got a fare?" Elise said, throwing the door open and getting out of the car.

"You two been up to something *rude*?" Todd said.

He was leering at her, his eyes settling on her breasts. He looked bigger close up, his stomach hanging over the top of his jeans, his face sinking into a double chin. She'd never liked him, even when he'd been mates with Andy. She stared coldly at a spot above his head while zipping her jacket up, packing herself away from him. Jason got out just as she heard her name being called from behind. She looked round and saw Carl coming across the top of the dunes, his hands in the pockets of his jacket.

"Hi!" she shouted, surprised, delighted.

Todd was smirking and Jason looked out of sorts. She turned and began to walk away. She didn't want Carl coming over and Todd saying something suggestive.

"See you later, Jase," she shouted, ignoring Todd.

She walked quickly. Carl had just stepped off the dunes and was stamping his feet on the tarmac to dust off the sand.

"Some kids said you'd walked this way. What you up to?" he said.

"Nothing much," she said.

"I've got a new DVD and Mum's going out. Fancy getting some food round my place?"

"Great," she said.

She took his arm and led him along the edge of the car park towards to the houses and town.

"What were you doing with them?" he said, nodding his head in the direction of Jason and his brother.

"Just having a laugh. You know me," Elise said.

SIX

Elise got up early, got dressed and stood in front of her bedroom mirror. She had a lavender T-shirt on over jeans. In her hand she had a lipstick that she had bought a couple of days before. It was a deep pink colour and she put it on carefully, going over it and then pushing her lips together to make sure it was evenly applied.

She took a critical look at herself. It was something she did from time to time. It often happened when she was feeling unsettled or anxious. Maybe it was because she hadn't seen much of Carl since the night they'd sat in his living room and watched a DVD, almost a week before. He'd been around, on the street, going into or coming out of a shop. He'd answered her daily texts. She'd even seen the garage lights on a couple of nights and assumed he'd been working on Andy's jeep. But they hadn't spent any real time together and she *missed* him.

She stood erect and stared hard at herself. She saw a serious-looking girl whose head was very still, whose expression was slightly haughty. She tried a smile but it felt wrong and immediately made her look younger. She straightened her mouth and ran her tongue over the lipstick. She had good skin. It was pale and smooth and she didn't blush or get freckles or spots. Her teeth were straight and white. Her hair was plain brown but it was thick and hung to her shoulders. Sometimes she scooped it up on top with combs or scrunchies; other times she let it hang or hooked it behind her ears. She had good hair. She knew that. From the chin up she was pleased with herself.

The rest was more of a problem. She was short, like her mum.

She sighed and backed away from the mirror. She riffled through her papers and began to pack her stuff for school.

When she was a child it had looked as though she would be tall. Her gran had been convinced of it. How often she had stood Elise in the middle of the room when her friends visited and asked them to admire her granddaughter's height and stature. Elise could remember being dressed up in some outfit her gran had put together for her, a frilly top maybe and short skirt; glittery tights and dancing pumps. *My lovely granddaughter takes after my side of the family. Tall and thin. Look at those legs. Sinew and muscle. Not a spare ounce of flesh. Dancing legs. You mark my word. She'll be following in my footsteps.* Gran teased Elise's skirt out and fluffed her hair up and put a record on while Elise danced around the room. Then she sat back, underneath the photographs of her younger self, and smiled with satisfaction as Elise did made-up ballet steps or disco dancing. *Oh, Elly, maybe you'll do better than I did. I'm not saying there's anything wrong with the End of the*

Pier show but it's not the West End of London! But when adolescence came, Elise stopped growing upwards and started filling out. Her gran smiled anyway. *Never mind, Petal; you've got a good brain. You'll always get by!* Not that Elise would have ever wanted to be a dancer. She'd stopped playing that game years before. But half a head taller, that would have been good.

The bedroom door opened and her mum came in. She was looking for something, picking things up and putting them down in a distracted way.

"What's up?" she said.

"Thought I saw my scent in here," her mum said.

"I put it back in your room," Elise said, glancing round.

Her mum had on a red roll-neck jumper and a short brown skirt and black tights. It looked odd. She let her eye run over her mum's shape. Her arms and legs were OK but her middle was chunky, like a sausage. And her breasts were jutting out like a shelf. In different clothes she could camouflage it.

"What are you staring at?" her mum said.

"Why don't you wear those black trousers?" she said.

"I like this skirt. And red suits me."

"But the black trousers make your legs look longer."

"I *like* this skirt," her mum said.

It was hard to believe that her mum and her gran had been related. When young, her gran had been tall and thin, with long legs and small breasts. Elise had seen professional photographs of her dancing days. She'd admired her glamorous looks and her fishnet tights and high-heeled dance shoes. Elise had only ever known her gran as an old lady with silver-white hair who had a wardrobe full of brightly coloured velour tracksuits. She was still tall, although her shoulders were rounded. When Gran got her pictures out she often looked critically at her daughter. *Your mum took after her father*, her gran told her. *He was shorter than me. He had to go on tippy-toes to get a kiss!*

"Oh, I nearly forgot!" her mum said, pulling Elise out of her thoughts. "Mr Palmer says you can do a couple of evening shifts next week. Four until eight, Monday and Tuesday. Sheila, who does them, is nearing her time..."

Her mum was going out of her room so she didn't have to answer. She went back to the mirror and looked at herself again. There was no getting away from the fact that she was top-heavy. Her breasts stretched her T-shirt. When she turned sideways her front jutted out. *You might not be tall but you've got a good figure*, her gran had said. *Men like something to get hold of!*

Elise pulled open her drawer and grabbed a pink cardigan. It was loose and let the colour of the T-shirt show through. She nodded. It looked better. For a second she stood up on her tiptoes, holding her shoulders straight. Why hadn't she taken after her gran?

She stood down. She was ready to go but something was still wrong. She put her face close up to the mirror. She pulled a tissue out of her pocket and wiped the lipstick off.

It was too pink.

At school she went to the library to work on one of the computers. After some time reading and typing and scooting round the Internet she sat back. Carl wasn't in school. He hadn't been in for days. That wasn't unusual. He'd wanted to leave at the end of year eleven and work as a builder with his dad. But Carl's mum wanted him to go to university. She was a manager in a restaurant in Norwich. She wanted Carl to get an education, to work with his *head* and not with his hands. There was a compromise. He agreed to stay on and do his A-levels and then make a choice. He was often absent, though, staying over his dad's and missing classes.

Elise knew why she had stayed on at school. She was in the sixth form for the same reason that most other kids were. There were no jobs. The teachers went on about preparing for university but it was all waffle. Elise wouldn't go to university; neither would most of the others who hung around the sixth-form block between classes. They were just treading water, biding their time, picking up a few more grades until they were old enough to work in one of the call centres around Norwich, or the shops in the new mall. Some of them, maybe Elise, would end up doing summer work in the cafés or restaurants, maybe even the hotels up along the Norfolk coast. Some people moved away, went to London. Andy had taken a route like that. He and Todd Bell had worked in Docklands laying computer cables for a couple of years. Then he joined the army for a proper career. At the time it had seemed like a good idea.

She took her hand off the mouse and sat back. She wondered what he was doing at that very moment; sitting in a cell? Or walking round a tiny exercise yard? She had no idea. The only thing she knew about prison life was what she saw in films or drama series. It had been the same when he was in Iraq. She used to wonder what he was doing there. She had pictured him marching through the desert or sitting on the back of a tank holding a rifle. When he came home he told her straight. *Sis, I spent most of my time guarding a roadblock, counting vehicles going by, keeping my eye on the helicopters above.* She had pictured him standing straight up like one of the sentries at Buckingham Palace, the shadow of a helicopter above him like a big black bird.

She logged off the computer, left the library and walked to the sixth-form common room. There were a couple of kids sitting up the far end. The bell for the end of lessons sounded and she went to her locker. She put her stuff in and pulled out a carton of juice. She walked towards the soft chairs. From behind she could hear the common-room door opening and closing and the level of noise increased as more people came in. When she sat down she noticed a tall blonde girl standing in the middle looking lost.

Elise stared at her. It wasn't anyone that she knew. She had dark blue trousers and a pink shirt on. Over the top she had a loose cardigan. Her hair was white blonde, short and spiky. She turned from side to side and then walked up to Gemma Collins, who was at her locker. Elise was close enough to hear.

"Hi," she said, with confidence, "I'm new. The secretary told me to come here and wait for the next session."

"New?" Gemma said.

Gemma was small and had frizzy hair that she was always trying to flatten with her hand. She looked up at the new girl, puzzled. Elise was surprised. A new kid in the sixth form? Why would anyone change schools so close to the final exams?

"I'm in 13A? Can you point me in the direction of the home room?"

"Home room?"

Elise raised her eyebrows. The new girl was American. Her accent was strong and her voice loud.

"Form room. Sorry, I meant form room!"

"I'm in 13A," Gemma said. "You can come with me."

"Oh, thanks. I thought you looked like a friendly face. I'm Sandy Miller."

"Gemma Collins."

The American girl placed her hand on Gemma's shoulder and patted it. Elise was struck by her forwardness. Gemma looked delighted. How typical of her. She was like a puppy, keen to be friends with anyone. The two of them walked out of the common room one behind the other, Gemma with her busy hair and the new girl as tall as a lamp post. No sooner had they gone when the door swung open and Carl appeared. He came straight over and flopped down in the next seat. He looked fed up, his shoulders down, his mouth in a pout.

"What's up with you?" she said.

"My mum got a call from Peacock. I'm two essays behind. Got to get one of them done by end of school today. Otherwise..."

"Want some help?"

"No, I'll crack on in the library."

"Hey, I've got something that'll cheer you up."

He raised his eyebrows.

"I bought it at great expense," she said, laughing, rummaging about in her bag.

"Really?" he said, shrugging, as if he wasn't interested.

"Let me see. Here," she said, holding a tube of sweets.

He managed a reluctant smile and took the packet.

"Wine gums. My favourite."

"Don't say I never buy you anything," she said, smiling.

He was quiet. It looked for a minute as if he was going to open the packet but then he slotted it into his jacket pocket.

"Done any more work in the café?"

"I will tonight. I'm taking down some of those old shelves. Fancy coming and giving me a hand?"

She caught his eye. He looked away. What did he mean? Was it that he wanted help with the shelves? Or was it a code?

"Let me think," she said, "am I free?"

"Come about seven. I'll have made a start by then."

She watched him go, his shoulders rounded, his bag hanging off his arm. When the door shut behind him the room felt empty. She upended her bag on to the seat beside her and began to sort her things. Some moments later she noticed that Jason Bell was sitting in the other seat. She frowned. She hadn't realized he was even in the common room. He leant towards her and whispered. His voice was so quiet she could hardly hear him.

"My brother's given me the keys for the BMW tonight. Want to meet me?"

She leant across until her mouth was close to his ear

"No thanks, I'm busy," she said in a tiny whisper.

"Tomorrow night? I'll still have the keys."

She left him sitting there and went out of the common room.

SEVEN

There had been times, in the past, when Elise thought that Carl might be her boyfriend.

She was eleven when he moved next door to her six years before. She'd been in the street with a friend as his family car pulled up ahead of the removal van. Michael got out with his arm around Penny, and Carl hung back, eyeing his new house with caution, his gaze moving around and settling on Elise. Elise had smiled politely but said nothing. Later when her gran told her mum about the new neighbours she'd said, *Black man married to a white woman? There'll be a few round here who won't like that!*

A few days later, she saw Carl in the playground, on his own. He was sitting on a bench opening a packet of sweets. She went straight up to him and introduced herself. A couple of other kids were with her and she told them he was her new neighbour. Then she plucked the packet from him and said, *Wine gums! My favourite!* He'd smiled at her, showing a mouthful of white teeth, the front ones slightly crooked. A couple of other kids came up, nosy, wanting to see who Elise was talking to. Carl seemed embarrassed by the attention. She took a sweet and handed the packet back to him. Then she noticed the colours of a football shirt underneath his school uniform. It was a vivid pink and blue. She put her hands up in mock horror.

"What football team do you support?"

"West Ham. Where I used to live."

"Oh no, round here we support local teams. Norwich or Man U."

He looked puzzled. When he saw she was joking he laughed.

That was the beginning of their friendship. Sometimes they walked to and from school together. They hung around with the same group of kids and often sloped off on their own. She went round his house, he came into hers. They often sat together in classes. There were always other kids around but because they lived next door to each other it was natural that they would spend time together.

Those early days were the first time that she thought they might be girlfriend and boyfriend. It was an innocent idea never properly formed. She pictured them walking together, holding hands, but that was the limit of what she imagined it to be. She knew that being a couple involved much more. She wasn't an idiot; she'd seen it in films and television and read about it in books but she didn't *know* it in her own body. At thirteen, when puberty crept up and took over, everything went into a kind of whirlwind. Then came strange, restless days when she retreated into friendships with her own sex. Carl did the same. She spent the time sitting in small groups listening to endless chatter about other kids, teachers, celebs, soap characters, clothes and anything else that raised an eyebrow and passed another hour. She saw a lot of Carl; how could she not? They lived next door to each other. But it was a distant nod or wave, a brief exchange of words, shoulders rubbing in the hallway as she took something in to his mum. Carl spent his time playing football or hanging round the streets. Sometimes he was down at the front, on the beach or at Marsh Park, on the edge of the town, where kids congregated if the weather was warm enough. Occasionally she saw a bunch of mates spilling out of his house after they'd spent the afternoon watching DVDs.

He shot up in height and she rounded out, her breasts putting a strain on every blouse she had. His voice became gravelly, sometimes squeaky, other times deep and throaty. She grew hair on her body and started her periods. She was embarrassed in his company, standing back from him in case they accidentally touched. He, conversely, seemed to get more relaxed as he got older, chatting and making jokes.

There were boys during that time, little skirmishes at discos or friends' houses, or down at the beach on dusky summer evenings. It started with dares or games of softball or lying around drinking from cans of beer. These couplings were quick, furtive, exciting. Like the cold beer they fizzed and intoxicated but had no lasting effect. The next day it was giggles and rude comments, people whispering in each other's ears and pointing across the refectory. *You snogged him!* They all did it. A snog with a boy was a collectable. It had no deeper meaning.

Carl did it too. She'd see him with his arm arced around the shoulder of some girl from another form, walking off towards the dunes, off into the comfortable darkness of the sand and the grasses.

When she was fifteen they began to spend a lot of time together again, walking on the beach, to Marsh Park, talking for hours on end, watching Carl's DVD collection. Not just Carl but the boys in general seemed to appear where the girls were, interested in them, ready to talk, ready to be more than friends. In those days she kept her eye on him; in his back garden, at the beach, on the games field, in the refectory at lunch time. He was tall with broad shoulders. His hair was black and he kept it short. It was as much as she could do not to reach out and run her fingers through it.

For the second time she wondered whether they might be boyfriend and girlfriend. She'd looked closely in her bedroom mirror, running her finger around her lips, wondering what a kiss from Carl would be like. Why couldn't they get together? It had happened to other kids. Boys and girls who'd ignored each other for years had started to pair off, walking to and from school, hanging round Marsh Park, tucked away in the corners of the bus shelter, curled around each other, so close you couldn't fit a piece of A4 paper between them.

He finally kissed her on the day of her sixteenth

birthday. He'd turned up at her front door about nine in the evening with a present, a DVD. Her mum was at work and she asked him if he wanted to come up to her room and see her new stereo. He followed her up the stairs. Once in her room she closed the door. Her bedside light was on and the room had a pink glow. The tiny stereo her mum had bought her was on her chest of drawers and she was about to point it out when Carl handed her the DVD. He'd wrapped it in glittery paper and on one corner was a ribbon bow. He shrugged in an embarrassed way and she said, *I wonder what this could be?* It was the first time he'd ever gone to such trouble. She pulled the paper off and saw that it was one of his favourite movies. *It's a classic*, he said. She went on tiptoes and kissed him on the cheek. As she moved away he bent down and kissed her other cheek. She stayed still, holding her breath, wondering what to do next.

He began kissing her on the mouth. Her neck was bent back and she was on tiptoes. He kept going for what seemed like ages; then they both stumbled towards the bed. In moments they were half sitting, half lying, sinking into each other, Carl kissing her softly and then with more force. He only stopped at the sound of the front door banging.

"Elly, you there? We're back."

It was her mum and her gran.

Later, when he'd gone home, she went back up to her room and saw that the covers on her bed were messed up. The sight of it excited her, made her feel jittery. At last.

They were together. She lay back on the bed and sent him a text.

It was a perfect birthday present, love Elly.

Getting undressed and ready for bed, she waited for the beep that told her she had a reply. She looked at her mobile to make sure that she had actually pressed the *send* button. After fifteen minutes or so she frowned. He must have gone to bed. She'd get a text from him in the morning.

But there was no text and she didn't see him at school. At lunch time she went out and headed for Marsh Park. It was hot and sunny and she was hoping that Carl might be around chatting to some mates. He wasn't. She almost turned heel and walked back the way she had come but she saw a group of kids from school sitting on the benches, so she went across. Jason Bell was there with his brother, Todd. Todd had his arm hooked around the neck of a girl called Sue Perkins, who had a diamond stud on the side of her nose. She was someone Elise didn't like. There were a couple of other girls and a boy who she didn't know very well.

"Have you seen Carl?" she said to Jason.

"Nope," Jason said.

"He didn't say he wasn't coming to school."

Although she said the words she was really thinking aloud. Sue gave a giggle and pulled a string of chewing gum out of her mouth.

"Didn't he ask your permission, Elly?" Todd said.

There was laughter and Elise swore. She should have

kept her mouth shut. She would go. There was no point in hanging round if Carl wasn't there. The group had no interest for her.

"I mean, it's not like you're his *girlfriend* or anything," Sue Perkins said, opening her mouth to show masticated gum.

Elise hesitated. On another day, another time, she would have had a pat answer, a put-down, a rebuff. But she said nothing. Sue exploded with glee.

"You? Carl's girlfriend? I don't think so!" she said.

Elise didn't have an answer. They were all looking at her. The boys had leaned forward, staring in her direction. The girls had perked up, sensing something of interest. Sue's eye was travelling up and down Elise's body. She could feel the girl's scrutiny like a searchlight, moving here and there and resting on her breasts. She turned to go and heard a ripple of laughter. Sue's voice was triumphant. "That's a laugh; she's not even in Carl's league!"

She didn't go back to school. She marched home, her throat knotted up. She went straight up to her room and lay face down on the bed. None of them knew about last night. She picked up the DVD from the bedside table. They'd watched it a couple of times over the years. *Everyone should have a copy of this movie*, he had said. No one knew he had given it to her. No one had seen her and Carl together in her bedroom, no one. She knew what had happened. Carl would know. That was what was important.

The front door sounded and she heard her gran's voice.

"Elly? You in?"

"I came home from school early," she shouted back. "I've got my period and I feel unwell."

"All right, love, anything you want, give me a shout."

She stayed in her room. Just after four o'clock she got a text.

I knew you'd like the DVD!

It was from Carl. He was answering the message she had sent him the previous night. Eighteen hours late. And he'd misread her words. She hadn't meant that the *DVD* was the best present – she'd meant him and her; the kisses; the *being together*. How had he not seen that? She sat up, an uncomfortable feeling taking hold of her. Had it meant nothing to Carl? Was it just like before, when they were all younger? The stuff that happened at parties? A snog with someone, anyone?

She stared at the text for a long while.

Maybe she wasn't the type he wanted for a girlfriend. How could she know what was going on in Carl's head? Was he like the others down at the park? Did he only see a short girl with heavy breasts? Someone to lark around with but nothing else? Her phone beeped again. It was another text from him.

I'm just going down the Beachcomber. Want to come along? I'm in the street.

She went out of her bedroom and into her mum's room at the front of the house. She stood by the curtains and peeked out of the window. Carl was there, down below. He was sitting on his garden wall with his back to her. His head was bent as if he was concentrating on something, his mobile maybe. Was he waiting for her to answer his text?

Looking along her street she saw Jason Bell and Sue Perkins coming along. Sue was shouting out something and Carl looked around at them. He stood up and walked across the road in their direction. The three of them stopped on the pavement opposite and started to chat.

She watched them with a feeling of gloom. What were they saying? *Elly was looking for you today. That girl, she never gives up. Why don't you tell her to get lost?* Was that what the conversation was about? Carl laughed out loud at something and Sue Perkins held her mobile out to him and then she laughed as well. What was she showing him? What was going on?

The three of them turned suddenly and walked away in the direction of the high street and the front. She watched Carl's back, in between Sue and Jason. He strode out as if he had somewhere he had to be. All the while she could see Sue Perkin's profile, her mouth moving non-stop. When they disappeared from sight she went back into her own room. She picked up her mobile. The screen was blank. No new message.

She began to pace up and down. She wasn't going to go to the Beachcomber. Let him see what it was like to not get an answer, to not know where *she* was.

Her room door opened and her gran was there.

"You all right, Petal?"

Elise managed a weak smile. She sat down on her bed and seconds later she was in tears.

"Oh, Elly! What's happened?"

Elise couldn't answer, just shook her head. Her gran sat down on the bed next to her. She was wearing a blue tracksuit and big white trainers that she'd bought from a charity shop. The legs of the tracksuit bottoms weren't quite long enough but Elise hadn't liked to say. She covered Elise's hand with hers. Her skin was cold even though it was a warm day. Elise looked down at the bony knuckles.

"What's up?" Gran said, her voice soft.

"It's just this boy I like," she said.

"Him next door?" Gran said.

"How did you know?"

"I'm not blind."

"I just don't know where I am with him. If he really likes me?"

"Oh, Elly. It's the oldest question in the world. *Does he love me?* Nobody's ever really sure."

"You! You had loads of boyfriends! You were famous!"

Gran had told her about all the men who used to come to the stage door with flowers and chocolates.

"But they weren't always the ones that I wanted, Petal," she said. "Sometimes the one I wanted didn't want me!"

Elise couldn't imagine this.

"You know what I used to do?"

Elise shook her head.

"Whenever I wasn't sure I used to step out with someone else. Didn't matter who he was, what he looked like, whether he had enough money to buy me a fish dinner or a gin and tonic. I just linked his arm and made sure the pair of us walked past the one I really wanted. Jealousy is a powerful emotion, Elly. It can make people do all sorts of things."

Later, when Gran had gone back downstairs, Elly lay on the bed and stared at the ceiling. After a while she pulled herself up and began to undress. She stood in the shower and let the hot water soak through her. After she was dry she snatched a hairbrush off the side and began to brush her hair rapidly, back off her forehead, her free hand grabbing it in a damp bunch. She shoved a scrunchie on and picked up some perfume and sprayed it on her neck. She got dressed and took a look in the mirror. Then she grabbed her mobile, went downstairs, called goodbye to her gran and left the house.

The Beachcomber Café was busy. There were loads of kids around, lounging on the sea wall, sitting on the beach, talking in small groups. Carl was standing among them. When she got closer she saw, on the periphery, Jason with Sue Perkins. She faltered for a second but kept walking, keeping her head up, a smile on her face.

Carl raised an arm to greet her.

"Hi," he said, "Dad was doing a job nearby so he picked me up this morning. I forgot my mobile!"

It was meant to be an explanation, she knew, and she smiled nonchalantly, avoiding looking in Sue Perkins' direction. Her eye settled on a tall, skinny boy who was a little away from the group bouncing a football off his knees. Peter Fenner.

"How does it feel to be a year older?" Carl said, cheerfully.

"Great," she said, looking at Peter, who was kneeing the ball into the air and catching it on the back of his ankle.

She went up to the counter and asked for a can of drink.

"I'll pay for that," Carl said.

"Thanks," she said, "I'll owe you one."

While he was getting his change she walked away from the group to where Peter was playing with the ball.

"Hi, Peter, what you up to?" she said, looking straight at him.

"Not much," he said.

"Want a drink?" she said, holding her can out.

"Cheers," Peter said, taking a gulp.

"Fancy going for a walk?" she said. "Over the sand dunes?"

"What?" Peter said, his forehead creasing up. "You having me on?"

His eyes flicked away from her in the direction of Carl and the others. He was about to blush. She could see the redness creeping up his neck. She sighed. She would have to spell it out for him. She put her hand on his arm so that he had to look back at her.

"Come on. You and me, in the dunes. We could have a sit-down somewhere."

It was a code. He knew it. She knew it. She pushed her chest out and played with her top button. He let the ball drop and roll away. She stepped across to him, stood on tiptoe and planted a kiss on his mouth, her tongue pushing at his lips. When she'd finished she threw a glance over at the others. They were all staring at her. In the middle Carl was looking puzzled. She turned away from them.

"Come on."

She took Peter's hand and pulled him in the direction of the sand dunes. As she was walking she could feel everyone's eyes on her back. When they got into the dunes she sat down almost immediately, lay back against the soft sand and began to unbutton her blouse.

She might not be Carl's girlfriend but this way everyone knew that it was her choice and not his.

EIGHT

Elise stood by the till in Palmer's while her mum read Andy's letter. She watched her mum's eyes travel from one side of the page to the other. When she got to the bottom Elise waited for her to comment. Her mum didn't speak, though; she sighed pleasantly and started at the top again. Elise rolled her eyes and looked at the time. It was ten past seven and she was due at the Beachcomber. She would be there now but the letter from Andy had been on the doormat when she got in from school and her mum had asked her to drop it into the shop so that she could read it.

Mr Palmer was hovering round the shelves rearranging cans and ticking things off a printout. He gave her a little smile. She waved back at him.

"Have you read this, Elly? Andy seems all right," her mum said.

She nodded. Of course she'd read it. It was a typical Andy letter. Short and sweet. *Dear Mum and Elly*, it started, *Things are not so bad. . .* and it went on for about twelve lines about his room, the food, the way he passed his days and at the end he put, *The appeal should happen in December or January, I can't wait. . .* It reminded Elise of the

letters they got when he was in Iraq. A page of short
wooden sentences about the camp, the weather, the flies,
the terrible food. At the end he would usually say how
long he had left – *Only six more weeks and I'll be home...*

She heard a cough and realized that Mr Palmer was
there beside them.

"Eveything all right, Sally?" he said, staring at the letter.

Elise disliked Mr Palmer. He was weedy and had the
whitest skin she had ever seen. It was as though he never
actually went out of his shop and into the daylight. His
hair was too dark, jet black, as if he used hair dye. He had
a sick wife who never came downstairs. There was an old-
fashioned green telephone on the counter, which her
mum said rang two or three times every shift. It was
always Rosemary, his wife, wanting to speak to Mr Palmer.
Elise had heard it once. The ring tone was low and shrill,
like an irritable bird.

The door opened and a customer came in. Mr Palmer
stood up straight. Her mum quickly folded the letter up
and gave it back to Elise and looked expectantly at the
customer. Elise left them there and went out, shoving the
letter into her pocket. She lowered her head and walked
into the driving wind towards the sea and headed for the
Beachcomber.

It was warm in the tiny café. She'd spread her leather
jacket on the floor and was sitting on it. Carl was alongside
her, reading Andy's letter. The heater was just centimetres
away from them and on the wooden floorboards sat two

half-drunk cans of warm lager. In the opposite corner was a pile of wood from the shelves they'd taken down. Outside, the wind blasted at the wooden walls. Further away was the sound of the sea twisting and turning. Carl handed her the letter back and she folded it and put it in her pocket. She drank some of the lager, her hands still tingling from handling the wood.

"That was hard work," she said, rubbing her palms together, feeling the grittiness of her skin.

"Place is falling down. I don't know why they don't just flatten it and build something new."

"Your dad could do it!"

"Never mind my dad, I could do it. Hey, you could help me. A couple of days and a skip would get rid of this shack. Then we could plan a new one. Build it in time for next summer."

"What about school? And exams?"

She was smiling. She'd heard Carl's schemes before. Buy a run-down house, do it up, make money. Buy a bigger one, do it up, make more money. They were daydreams. Sometimes they lasted all day long.

"We could go into business together. Murdoch Renovations."

"You mean, Murdoch and Hanson Renovations."

"That's too much of a mouthful."

"We could have headed note paper. Or even a website," she said, joining in with the game.

"You could project-manage. I could do the building work," he said, nudging her.

"That means I'd be in an office all the time! That's not fair."

"You're a woman. Women don't do building work."

"Yes they do!"

"OK, I'll get Dad to teach you some stuff. How do you feel about being a plasterer? Or a chippie?"

She laughed, imagining herself in builder's overalls, her hair pulled back and a pencil behind her ear. She shook her head. She just couldn't see it. She noticed then that the music had stopped so she opened the CD player and took out the silver disc, putting it away carefully in its plastic box. She put another one in to play. Moments later the café was filled with the sound of girls singing in harmony.

She leaned back against the wall and sat quietly. Their conversation had run its course and she didn't feel any need to talk for the sake of it. They were sitting centimetres apart but they weren't touching. They hadn't touched since that night a couple of weeks before when they'd been clearing out the larder and found a nest of mice. That's how it went with them. Every few months there was something that drew them together, a kind of magnet. It happened when they were alone. There was some spark, some trigger and they fell towards each other, hungrily, easily. The next day it was as if it had never happened. She remembered each time, though, every single one, as if she'd written it in a diary.

The track changed. A slow, bluesy song came on with a saxophone playing. It filled the tiny café with a swooning sound. Carl picked up his can and drank from it. The notes of the music were smooth as silk, the girls' voices sliding along on top of it. Beside her, she could feel Carl swallowing back the lager.

"So I hear you and Jason got together?" he said, after a while.

She looked round at him.

"Jason and you?" he repeated.

She shrugged and tucked her leather jacket around her legs. Even though the heater was on there was a draught from somewhere, a thin, icy needle of air coming from a gap in the boards.

"I didn't think he was your type."

"He's not. He's definitely not my type," she said, frowning.

"It's just that you never said," he said.

"You know me!" she said, sighing. "It was nothing. I was just passing time."

He didn't answer. Elise tried to think of something to say. Instead she tapped out the beat of the song on her knee. There was an atmosphere in the café which was odd. It wasn't the first time that one of them had been with other people. Elise had spent time with a couple of lads, but they were fleeting things, a few kisses, a couple of meetings, no more than that. And Carl had had girlfriends. There'd been at least two that Elise knew of who had been keen on him. He'd hung around them and for a while it had sent her into a panic but none of it had lasted long. No more than a week or so.

"You should be careful, though. There might be talk."

"What about?"

"About you and him. In the car."

"What about me and him?"

"About stuff that you do."

"What did he say?"

She was suddenly irritated. She sat up, reached across to the CD player and turned it off. There was a moment's silence; then, from outside, she could hear the water hitting the shingle.

"It's nothing to do with me," Carl said, standing up, brushing his jeans, moving across to the sink, lining up some empty drink cans that were there.

"What?" she said, standing up, pulling at his arm. "What did he say?"

He shook his head, "That you got up to *stuff*. In the back of the BMW."

"What stuff?" she said, half laughing, half indignant.

He shrugged and looked away, his hand fiddling with the tap, turning it on and off for no reason.

"Just be careful," he mumbled. "You don't want to end up with a kid."

She looked at him with astonishment. What did he think she got up to? Did he think that she was *easy*?

"What?" he said, looking embarrassed.

"I know how to look after myself!"

She was annoyed; she was more than that, she was angry. Why did she have to defend herself? It was her business what she did.

63

"That's all right then," he said, managing a half smile.

He picked up the two cans from the floor. He handed one to her, his fingers brushing against hers. Elise took it roughly and plonked it on the side. She didn't care what people thought of her. Except for Carl. He should know the truth about her.

"You know I don't. . ." she started.

I don't have sex with boys because I'm waiting for you, she wanted to say, but a sudden bang on the shutters made her look round.

"What?"

Carl stepped back. There was another bang, then another. The shutters wavered as more things hit them. For a second it felt like they were being attacked, shot at. Then it stopped and she could hear voices from outside, kids shouting out and running away.

Carl's face was angry, his hand in a fist. "Throwing stones! Stupid kids!"

Elise turned away, her words lost in the drama. She tidied up the CDs and put her leather jacket on. He had his back to her. He was fastening the shutters again, making sure they were tightly closed. The moment for talking had passed. It wasn't the right time to say what she wanted to say. She changed the subject.

"There's some new girl in 13A. Funny-looking with stiff blonde hair."

"New? In the upper sixth?" Carl said, turning the lights off and plunging the café into darkness before opening the door. He stepped out and looked around; Elise followed.

A gust of wind from the sea pulled her hair back and sent cold air up her nose and into her ears. She pulled the leather jacket tightly around her.

"She's American. Her dad's got a job at the uni so they're living here for a year. She's going to do A-levels. That's what Gemma said. I think she's pretty rich."

Carl was fixing the padlock on to the door.

"I haven't seen her," he said, grunting, trying to get the lock to click shut.

"Her name's Sandy something. Sandy Miller, that's it. You can't miss her, she's about six foot tall!"

"She won't like it here. It's not exactly California," Carl said.

"Yeah. Bet she doesn't last two weeks," Elise said.

They turned away from the sea, their shoulders rounded against the cold, and headed back towards the houses. After a few metres Elise slipped her hand through Carl's arm and leaned into him.

"Hanson and Murdoch Limited," she said. "That's the best name for the company."

"We'll be millionaires before we're twenty-five."

Elise sighed. It was a nice daydream.

NINE

Sandy Miller fitted in quickly. The American girl settled easily and there was hardly anyone who didn't seem to know about her. Elise was unimpressed by the flutter of interest she had caused. Everywhere she went there was a conversation going on about the new girl. She tried to avoid it and sat apart from the other kids in the common room, reading her book, *Death of a Salesman*. It was a text that she was studying for English literature. She had finished the first act and was just starting the second. Around her kids were talking about Sandy Miller.

"Her parents come from Connecticut; that's, like, north of New York."

"Her mum and dad are rich."

"She could have gone to St Benedict's."

"They wanted her to experience a British state school."

"She calls everything British. Like, I like your *British* movies. I like your *British* bands. I like *British* weather."

"Wait till she feels the sea wind."

"She lives next to the coast in Connecticut. She says they have to dig their way out of the snow for months!"

"I like her. She's not stuck-up like some Americans."

"You don't know any Americans!"

"On TV, I mean. Those Americans."

Elise sighed. Sandy Miller was the talk of the sixth form. Whenever the girl walked into the common room there was a murmur as various kids shuffled about, their interest aroused by this beanpole with white hair.

She looked down at *Death of a Salesman* again. She was supposed to have read the second act by that afternoon. She couldn't concentrate, though. She was thinking about the theatre trip to Norwich on Thursday, when they were going to see the play. She and Carl had seats together. And they would sit together on the coach there and back.

It was time, she thought, for something to happen between them. It had been weeks since there had been anything. Every time she saw him she wanted to reach out and touch his face, stroke his arm, edge herself close enough so that she fitted up against him, her head flat against his chest. It hadn't happened, though, and she was afraid that this tenuous thing between them would fizzle out, fade away.

She thought about the silly conversation that had started in the Beachcomber weeks before about them setting up a company together. It had carried on during the evenings when she'd been helping him with other things. It was jokey and light. A make-believe game. Yet it had laid the seeds of an idea inside her. An image of the two of them together in the future. Why couldn't they work together? He could work with Michael for a couple of years and she could get temporary jobs. Between them they could save up some money. Enough to get a loan from a bank and start a small business. Maybe, during that time, something *proper* would start between her and Carl. Something deep and life long. She wouldn't have to be his girlfriend in the soppy way that other kids were; swapping bracelets, wearing each other's clothes, saying *me and Bobby* or *me and Jack* every time any topic of conversation came up. But if they could just be together, their relationship could grow. She imagined it like climbing plants, the tendrils winding round and round each other until they were intertwined.

The bell for the change of lessons was ringing and she looked up from her book. The common-room door was opening and closing and people were moving about. One day she and Carl would be lovers. They would. The thought of it gave her a delicious tingle across her chest, making her skin rise up.

Gemma had sat down a couple of seats along from her. She was talking to another girl and she caught Elise's eye, as if she were trying to draw her into the conversation. Elise looked back to her book and turned a couple of pages, her eyes staring down at the paper as though she were engrossed in what she was reading.

"Sandy doesn't dye her hair. That's her natural colour. She's not albino or anything, she's just got this amazing blonde hair. She said her mum's the same. If I was her I'd grow it!"

"Or get extensions," the other girl said.

"I mean, she could go to a private school but she's come here! Would you come here if you could go somewhere like St Benedict's?"

"They're all stuck-up there."

"That's because they're all rich!"

"That shows what a *nice* person Sandy is. Coming here."

Elise snapped her book shut. She was not interested in this girl from America who should have gone to St Benedict's. She gave Gemma a look of impatience but the girl didn't notice. She was pulling at her frizzy hair as if trying to straighten it. No wonder she was overwhelmed by the beanpole.

The common-room door opened and Sandy Miller came in, a couple of girls behind her talking rapidly. She marched across and sat in the seat in between Elise and Gemma.

"Hi!" she said, brightly. "You know what? Some guys have pushed paper down the sink in the restroom. There's water all over the floor!"

Restroom. It was one of the many American phrases that she used which amazed everyone.

"Oh! She calls trainers, *sneakers*!"

"And rubbish is *garbage*."

"We were walking to the bus stop the other day and her mobile rang and she called it her *cell phone*!"

Everyone was so impressed by this girl. Elise huffed silently. Anyone would think that she was a creature from Mars, not a girl from another country. She heard Sandy Miller's voice in her ear and was startled to feel the girl's hand fleetingly on top of hers. She looked up, surprised that she was being spoken to.

"Pardon?" she said, withdrawing her hand.

"I'm reading *Death of a Salesman* too!"

Elise nodded and gave a thin smile. She had to. Sandy Miller's face was like a huge sun glowing in front of her.

"I'm joining the English Lit class after half-term."

"That's good," Elise said, trying to hold on to the smile.

"Hey!" Gemma said, sitting up straight, looking pleased with herself. "You're not related to Arthur Miller, are you?"

Sandy laughed, her fingers like a rake combing through her hair until it stood bolt upright on her head. Then, with the palm of her other hand, she patted it all down.

"No! There are an awful lot of Millers in the States."

"I knew that. I was only kidding," Gemma said.

Elise noticed that Gemma's neck had gone red. She really had thought it.

"I have to go," Elise said.

The library had to be quieter. Maybe if she forced herself she could get more of the book read. Sandy leant towards her, her shoulder touching Elise's.

"Isn't Miller great? I read this in, like, three or four sittings!"

Elise mumbled a reply, picked up her bag and slotted the book in.

The library was full of year sevens. Elise looked around with dismay. She walked off along the corridor and found an empty classroom. Sitting in the back corner she opened the book. She had under an hour to read the second act. If she scanned a lot of it she could probably manage.

Her mum was standing at the kitchen sink holding the wall calendar in her hand. She was looking at it in a distressed way. Elise pulled out a chair and sat down, her whole body deflating.

"I didn't realize the prison visit was the same day as your play," her mum said.

Elise couldn't speak.

"I know you wrote it on the calendar but I didn't match them up. Here it is. *Trip to see Miller*."

"It's been booked for weeks!" Elise said.

"I know, I'm sorry. I didn't write the prison visit on the calendar, perhaps I should have..."

"Wasn't there another day to visit Andy?"

"They just sent a letter. It had a date on it. I didn't write it on the calendar because I knew I wouldn't forget it. I've been looking forward to it..."

Why did her mum mess things up? Couldn't she get anything right?

"I could go and see him on my own? I could tell him that you had to go to see the play? For your exams?" her mum said.

"No! You can't do that! How would he feel?"

"He'd be OK about it."

"I can't," she said, standing up, pushing the chair under the table with force. "I can't not go and see him."

"Andy would understand."

Elise knew that. She knew Andy wouldn't mind. *Hey, sis, you look after your education. That's what important.* He would think of her welfare, her future. And all she was thinking of was spending an evening with Carl.

"The play'll be on for a while. Tell you what. I'll buy two tickets; then you and I can go and see it together," her mum said.

She almost laughed. Her mum watching an Arthur Miller play. The two of them in the theatre together.

"It doesn't matter," she said, tersely, "I'll tell the teacher. Maybe someone else will use the ticket."

Her mum replaced the calendar on the wall. "You never know. You might get a refund," she said.

At a little after seven she stepped out of her house and closed the door crossly behind her. She pulled her leather jacket tight. She headed for the front, closing her lips and screwing up her eyes against the wind. Why did the prison visit have to be on the same day as the theatre trip? How could she be so unlucky?

The tide was in. It was too dark to see it but Elise could hear it pummelling the beach as she turned on to the sea wall. A few seconds later the spray hit her face and she moved to the side and pulled her collar up high. Of course she could not go and see Andy. He wouldn't mind, he'd understand. And she could go next time. But even thinking like this gave her an unpleasant feeling. A curdle of guilt in her stomach. How could she choose a theatre trip over a visit to her brother, who she hadn't seen for weeks? She glanced up. Ahead she could see bars of light coming from the Beachcomber. She quickened her step, half running towards the café. It just wasn't fair. A trip out of Colby East with Carl. Something she'd looked forward to for ages. Now she couldn't go. She pushed the Beachcomber door open and stepped inside to get out of the cold. Then, using force, she pulled it sharply so that it banged shut. Carl looked up. He was squatting down, pulling nails from the floorboards. She stood stiffly in the bright café, the heat creeping up her legs. He pushed himself up and faced her. Her mouth was twitching with annoyance.

"What's up?" he said.

"I've got to go with Mum on Thursday to visit Andy. It means I'm going to miss the theatre trip."

"This Thursday?" he said, feeling the floor with his foot, his concentration not really on her.

"The trip to see *Death of a Salesman*. I've been looking forward to it!"

"News to me. I thought you hated the play."

"But the trip was different. Going out. Out of town. To Norwich."

"It's hardly bright lights, big city."

She stopped. Norwich was nothing to him. He spent lots of time there with his dad. He didn't get it. It wasn't the play or the place, it was going with him, but how could she tell him that?

"Where did you say Andy was?"

"His prison is in Essex. We have to get a bus and then a

train to London, then a train out to Essex. We'll be travelling all day for an hour's visit! It's a real pain."

"He'll be looking forward to it."

"If it wasn't this Thursday..."

She felt like stamping her foot with annoyance. Carl had knelt down on the floor again and was feeling the planks with his fingers. He'd lost interest. He didn't seem at all bothered that she wasn't going on the theatre trip. Would he even notice if she slipped out the door and off into the night? Did he even care if she was there or not?

"You can tell Andy that I've done a lot on the jeep. That should cheer him up."

"Um..."

"Hand us those big pliers, will you."

The wind hit the shutters, making a booming sound. It loosened the window fastenings and Carl leapt up, reached across and pulled them tight.

"This place is like a house of cards..." Carl said.

She didn't answer. Her face felt like it was set in cement. Carl stepped across and put one arm around her shoulder.

"Cheer up, mate. Look on the bright side. At least you don't have to sit through the play," he said.

She nodded, feeling his hand squeezing her arm.

"Give us a smile, partner," he said, "and I'll give you a present."

Her mouth pulled into a small smile and she nudged him away.

"Where's my present?" she said.

He handed her a giant pair of pliers. "You want to be a part of Murdoch Construction, you have to work for it."

She took the heavy tool and sighed. "I think you mean *Hanson and Murdoch Construction*," she said.

On Thursday morning she and her mum left about ten. There were a dozen or so other people on the bus and her mum started to talk to a couple of women she knew. Elise looked forlornly out of the window at the grey town and the empty streets. Passing her school, she felt her throat warm up with emotion. At four-fifteen the coach would be in the car park. Everyone would file on to it and then it would set off, for Norwich, to see the play. Her teacher had managed to sell her ticket. There wouldn't even be an empty seat to remind people that she wasn't there.

TEN

It wasn't an old-fashioned prison surrounded by a high brick wall. It was a honey-coloured brick building that stood out in the Essex countryside. From a distance it looked more like a modern hospital or school. When they got closer Elise picked out the high wire fence that stood around it. There were no towers and no guards with guns. Just a line of CCTV cameras around the top of the fence.

The bus was hot, the windows steamed up with the collective breath of the passengers. The closer they got the more noise there was. She heard voices from behind her saying, *Nearly there! Not long now!* There was the sound of children becoming excited, their feet banging, one or two running up the aisle even though the driver had given strict instructions for everyone to stay in their seats belted up. Now and then, through the voices, she could hear the notes of a recorder rising and falling like some misplaced bird.

Her mum gave her a tired smile. She returned it. They were getting near to seeing Andy. The first time since the court case.

They got out of the bus, thirty or so women and

children. There were also a couple of elderly men. Elise wondered if they were fathers of inmates. Then she thought about their father, Edward Hanson. He had no idea that his son was in prison. Would he care? Did he even remember that he had two children? It was on the tip of her tongue to say something to her mum about it, but then she thought, why bother?

The land around the prison was flat as far as the eye could see. The sky was low with cloud and there was a feel of dampness in the air. Elise and her mum followed the adults, all walking sombrely, in contrast to the children, who were hopping along, three or four skipping ahead. Behind her was the child with the recorder, a boy of about seven who was wearing an Arsenal tracksuit and looked cold. He held the recorder high and seemed to be playing it, although Elise couldn't make out whether there was a tune or not. A high gate, wide enough for a lorry to get through, slid open and the visitors walked through. A prison officer directed them to a one-storey building inside the compound and they queued outside. It looked like a couple of Portacabins that had been joined together. Inside, the queue seemed to move quickly. Elise could see X-ray machines for the visitors' bags and metal-detector gates to walk through. It was like the airport except no one was going on holiday. Elise turned her back on the whole thing. She put her hands in her pockets and closed her eyes. A child was screaming at the top of its voice because it didn't want to go through the gate on its own. *Come on, Bobby! Else you won't be able to see Dad!* Further on, by the exit door, there were prison officers with dogs.

Twenty minutes later they were sitting across a table from Andy. He looked thinner.

"Prison keeps the weight down. That's not such a bad thing," he said, cheerfully.

He had a cut over one eye that had a butterfly stitch across it.

"It's nothing," he said, "I just had to work something out with an old soldier along my balcony. A veteran of Northern Ireland who thinks he knows it all."

"What about the appeal?" her mum said. "What does Mr Joseph say?"

"He's hopeful. He says the judge was just trying to make an example. As soon as we get a hearing date they should at least halve the sentence. With good behaviour I could be out end of January."

"That would be brilliant," Elise said.

Andy was smiling. While her mum was talking about things that had happened back home, she ran her eye over him. Although he had lost weight, he had jowls on his face, pulling it down, giving it a hangdog look. His prison sweatshirt looked faded with washing and she saw a stain on the front, as if some food had dribbled down. How different to when he was at home. Constantly worrying about his appearance, ironing his shirts, polishing his shoes. It was one of the things he'd liked, *loved* about the army. Being smart, looking good, having everything in its place.

Just across the aisle, a couple of tables away, she noticed the young boy in the Arsenal tracksuit. He had his recorder up to his mouth and was going through the scales. When he finished a couple of people around gave him a little clap. The prison officers stayed stony-faced.

Andy produced a plastic bag from his pocket and began to roll up a cigarette, pulling at a small bundle of tobacco and easing it into a straight line on top of a cigarette paper. Elise noticed that he had three roll-ups already made.

"You could give up smoking while you're in here. That would be a good thing!" her mum said.

Andy took a deep breath. His mouth was closed and he drew air in through his nose. He was irritated. Elise knew what he felt like. Her mum just rattled on and on, saying the first thing that came into her head.

"Mum, these smokes, this tobacco is the *only* thing that keeps me from going mad in here. If it wasn't for this they'd come to my room one morning and find me hanging from the ceiling by my belt."

Her mum looked shocked and her hands flew up. Elise grabbed hold of her arm. Andy began to backtrack immediately.

"I'm joking, I'm joking. I just like a smoke. You know that!"

Her mum looked as though she was going to cry. She took a couple of moments searching her pockets and then pulled out a bundle of tissues and blew her nose.

"Mum, Mum! I was making a joke. It's called graveyard

humour. You make fun out of the worst possible things. That's how we get by! Like in Iraq. You should have heard the jokes there."

Her mum continued to wipe her nose. Elise gave Andy a look of exasperation. *Now look what you've done!* she mouthed, and he reached across and took hold of his mum's hand. Elise felt the tension ease as he carried on apologizing and chatted about the things he was doing. In the back of her head she could hear the notes of the boy's recorder, rising up. It sounded sad, each note climbing on the other.

After a while, when her mum had cheered up, Andy sat back.

"I need you to do me a favour. You or Elly, go into my wardrobe. At the bottom there's a blue shoebox? It's got photos and stuff in it. On the top there *should* be a packet with some shots of me in Iraq. Or they might be in one of my drawers. Post them to me. I want to show them around."

"OK," Elise said.

While her mum was telling Andy about people in Palmer's, Elise looked across at the clock on the far wall. The numbers 15.51 showed. Had a whole hour gone by since they'd sat down? What had she actually said to him? Hardly anything that she could remember. All small talk, nothing of any importance.

Andy was talking about a book he was reading on classic cars.

"My jeep? It's a Wrangler 1987. The first year they

started to make that model. It'll be worth a lot of money when I've finished fixing it. I might take it to the auction. It could make me a nice sum. Or I could start collecting old American cars.."

"Or you could put it on eBay!" she said, grinning.

Andy gave a laugh. Elise knew that he was used to her mocking him for his attachment to eBay.

"How's school, sis?" he said.

"All right. Some new girl's started. An American," she said. "Boffin type."

"Not brainier than you, though?"

"Course not," Elise said.

"Make sure you get those exams. Don't end up like me."

"Oh, Andy, don't say that," her mum said.

"You're not in here because you didn't get your A-levels," Elise said.

"Look around, Elly; you don't see many doctors or accountants or teachers in here."

Her mum started to talk about the journey: how they got there, which trains they took, how they had to find the right platform when a train was cancelled. Elise thought about what Andy had said as she kept her eye on the clock. 13.57, 13.58, 13.59. She looked around the visiting room. There were a lot of black faces as well as white. She wondered what lives they had left behind. Was there a place there for them to return to when they got out? She felt full of emotion suddenly, her throat dry and crackly. Andy had a place in their lives. An Andy-shaped space that he could slot back into. How many of the others had that?

A voice burst out from a nearby table. "Tell him to put that bloody recorder away. I'm sick to death of it!"

Instantly a prison officer moved into the seating area, determination in his face. Elise swung round to see what was going on and saw the boy with the recorder backing away from the table.

"Don't be like that, Terry. He just wants to show you what he's learned," a woman said.

One of the officers stood squarely behind the man called Terry at the same time as a shrill bell sounded. Elise stared at the little boy. His face had clouded over, his mouth bunched up. He had his hands behind him. When he turned and walked towards the door she could see the recorder flat against his back. The woman was still talking.

"He'll have the hump all the way home now."

The bell seemed to get louder, drowning out any last words. Elise stood up and stepped towards Andy, hooking him round the neck and kissing his cheek. She couldn't say anything in case she cried. Her mum, who had been close to tears a couple of times, was composed, and gave Andy a peck and told him to look after himself. They made their way to the exit. By the time they had sidestepped all the tables and chairs Andy had gone.

The bus was waiting for them outside.

"Apart from that scratch on his head he seemed all right, didn't he?" her mum said, when the bus finally moved off and was racing across the empty countryside.

Elise nodded just to please her. Then she looked back up the coach. The boy in the red tracksuit was sitting a couple of rows behind, his face red, his nose running, wiping his tears away with the back of his hand.

ELEVEN

They got home from the prison visit just after eight. Elise stood with her back to the radiator, letting her knuckles rest on the hot metal. The warmth wafted up through her clothes.

"I could get some soup out of the freezer? Or fry up some bacon and eggs?" her mum said.

Elise shook her head. She wasn't hungry. She went upstairs, her feet heavy. The journey and the visit had drained her. She went to the toilet and then washed her hands. When she came out of the bathroom she stood for a moment outside Andy's room door. She hadn't been in his room since he'd gone into prison. She turned the handle and pushed it open and clicked on the light. There were no surprises. It was just as he'd left it on the day he went to court, tidy and clean. The bed, which edged on to the wall, was perfectly made, the duvet neatly puffed up. The chest of drawers and chair and desk were free of clutter. His laptop sat closed and mute, a pile of books next to it, all with covers showing swords and guns and military uniforms. She walked across to his wardrobe. The doors were shut and she knew that if she opened them she would find his suits hanging under polythene bags, his shirts ironed on hangers, his ties laced over a rail, lined up, ready to march off.

Then there was the memorabilia.

Each wall was covered in things that Andy had found or bought during his years in the army. There were berets and shirts and flags. There were badges and belts and ties. There was even a miniature Swiss bayonet mounted on the wall. The room was crammed with stuff and yet it was all perfectly orderly, each item pinned or hung neatly, the walls a kaleidoscope of military colours, looking exotic and yet so very English.

Andy loved this stuff.

She remembered then the photos of Iraq he wanted. She was too tired to get them, though. She'd do it in the morning. She turned the light off and closed the door. From downstairs she could hear the sound of the television and her mum making cooking noises in the kitchen. It was almost eight-thirty.

The play would have been on for an hour. *Death of a Salesman* by Arthur Miller. She hadn't even liked it. An old bloke falling apart, messing up his family. A father driving his sons mad. A husband cheating on his wife. What did it have to do with her? She was seventeen, her brother in prison. She was in love with the boy next door but she couldn't bring herself to tell him. Why wasn't there a play about someone like her?

It hadn't really mattered what play they had gone to see. It was the trip itself that was the thing. In Norwich they would have had a couple of free hours and the teachers would say *Don't go into any pubs* and they would nod and say yes but that was the first thing they would do. Find a pub. Have a few drinks. Have a laugh. Get to the theatre in the nick of time. Nudge each other and whisper through the performance if they could get away with it. And on the way home she would sink into a doze beside Carl.

And she had missed it.

In her own room she stood in front of her long mirror. Her hair was flat from the damp air outside. She took her leather jacket off and looked at her body. Her breasts sat out, stretching the wool of her jumper. She sighed and sat down on the edge of her bed and lay back. She put the palms of her hands across her middle. It was the only time when her stomach was completely smooth and flat. Even her breasts seemed smaller, less bulbous, less in everyone's face. It was nice. It was the person she was meant to be. The person in her head. Elise Hanson, a little taller, a little thinner. More like her gran than her mum.

An image of her gran formed in her head. Gran's long legs that seemed to stretch from her feet to her shoulders. Even that wasn't tall enough for her because she wore the highest heels. *How did you dance in those, Gran?* Elise had asked her when she was small, when Gran used help her dress up in dance clothes. *You can get used to anything, Petal*, she had said, delicately fingering the straps of the only pair she had left.

Elise lifted her feet up in the air. Her boots hung there, heavy and masculine. Maybe she should buy some high-heeled shoes. Lots of people wore them. She struggled up into a sitting position and pulled the boots off. Then she lay back. She was feeling tired. Even though she was fully dressed and her room light was still on she turned on her side and closed her eyes. After a while she drifted off to sleep.

When she woke up it was dark and her duvet was over the top of her. She sat up, wearily, not quite sure why she'd been lying there in her clothes, and then remembered. Her mum must have turned the house lights off and gone to bed herself. They'd both been travelling all day. No wonder she had drifted off to sleep. She looked at her watch. It was still only ten to eleven.

She turned on her bedside lamp and the room filled with a pink glow. The coach would be arriving back from Norwich soon. She remembered the consent letter. *Please arrange for the students to be met at approximately eleven fifteen.* She pictured the words on the page. There were two drop-off points, she recalled, one in school and one at the bus turning-circle in town. Carl would get off there, soon, in twenty minutes or so. What if she went to meet him, to hear all about the play, to tell him about her visit to see Andy? She pushed back the duvet. Why not? She sat up, wide awake, stretching her arms. She stood up and straightened her clothes. She put her boots on and grabbed the brush and pulled it through her hair several times. Her mouth felt dry so she went into the bathroom and brushed her teeth. She went back into her room and picked up a lipstick. She held it up to her lips for a second, then changed her mind, chucking it sideways on to the bed. On her way downstairs she zipped up her leather coat, checked that she'd picked up her mobile and her keys and went out of the house, closing the front door quietly behind her.

It was foggy but she could see ahead, the yellow street lights blurry and vague. She walked quickly, her hands in her pockets, her head down. It was a route that she did two or three times a day, maybe more. She could have done it blindfolded.

It would be a surprise for Carl. He was probably fed up with all the lads on the trip. Knowing them they were telling rude jokes, being sick or having farting contests. He would be glad to see her. A fresh face would cheer him up.

She came out of the backstreets and on to the main road. She walked away from the sea towards the bus stop. Ahead she could see the sidelights of a couple of cars; parents waiting to pick up their kids. She looked into the brightly lit up minicab office. Inside, among a group of men, she could see Todd Bell, lounging in an armchair, his big stomach sticking out, a can of drink in his hand. She passed on until she got to the doorway of the Chinese takeaway. The shop was closed but there was some light from the neon sign above it.

She waited.

Moments later she could see a glow in the distance, the fog swirling, the coach emerging through, its lights bright and sharp against the murky blackness. She smiled, feeling pleased with herself for being there. The people in the cars across the way were pointing towards the coach. She walked up and down in the small shop entrance, stamping her feet, feeling the cold nibbling at her toes.

The coach pulled up. It looked almost empty. Most kids would have got off at school. It wheezed as it came to a halt and the side door swung open automatically. The internal lights went on and it was lit up like a stage. She peered out of the doorway. She decided against walking up to the coach and showing herself. She wanted to surprise Carl. She'd wait until he disembarked and walked past the Chinese.

Some kids got off the coach. They crossed the road to the cars. She could hear someone, the coach driver, probably, shouting out for people to get a move on. Carl was taking his time. Most likely he'd fallen asleep. Bored and fed up, without her to talk to, he'd dozed off and slept the whole journey. A couple of boys burst out of the coach, talking at the tops of their voices, laughing rudely at something. Then the American girl got off. The beanpole, her white hair catching the light. Elise remembered then that the teacher had sold her ticket off at the last minute. The American must have bought it. She rolled her eyes to herself.

Carl got off next. He stopped for a second and stretched his arms up to the sky. She'd been right, he had been sleeping. A couple of girls got off behind him and then the door of the coach slid closed. The girls said something she couldn't hear and walked off across the road towards the other car. The coach started to reverse. She could hear the beep, beep, beep of its indicator. The beanpole was still standing on the pavement and was saying something to Carl. *Come on!* she thought. *Come on.*

She was as tall as Carl and she was doing that thing with her hand, combing it through her hair and making it stand on end, like straw. Carl said something and she laughed. The coach swung round the turning-circle, its headlights sending great beams of yellow light into the fog. When it had turned the street was darker, only a glow from its rear lights.

"Come on!" Elise whispered the words.

But they didn't move. The American girl reached across to Carl's shoulder and brushed something away. He was perfectly still and looked down as she did it. Then she stood still, facing him. Elise stared at the pair of them. There was space between them. They weren't touching. Even so, she found herself holding her breath, her eye on Carl, then back to the girl, her stupid hair standing on end, then back to Carl again.

He lowered his head suddenly and Elise felt her whole chest lurch. Was he going to *kiss* her? But he angled his face down to her ear and stayed there for a few seconds. He must have said something because she laughed out loud. Elise sunk back into the doorway. She heard a car horn beep lightly from somewhere; she couldn't work out which direction it came from. In moments a silver car glided past the Chinese takeaway towards the coach. She looked out. It came to a halt by the bus stop. The

American girl pulled open a door. She said "Bye" and got in.

The car drove off and Carl stood for a few moments until its lights had disappeared. Just as he turned she stepped as far back into the doorway as she could. She stood completely still, hoping that he would cross the road and walk on the other side.

He did.

She let him pass. She didn't want him to see her, to know that she'd waited for him.

TWELVE

She woke up to darkness on Friday morning. She turned over towards the window and shut her eyes tightly. After a few moments she rolled the other way, pulling her duvet up so that it almost covered her head. Eventually she opened her eyes and looked at the clock. It read 4.52. She lay on her stomach, her face into the pillow.

She couldn't sleep.

She sat up. It was cold in the bedroom. It was too early for the central heating. She got out of bed and grabbed her dressing gown. She wrapped it tightly round, her arms and shoulders stiffening with the chill air. It would be hours before her mum was up. She went to the toilet. Washing her hands, she stared at herself in the bathroom mirror. Her eyes looked puffy and her lips dry.

She thought of Carl the previous evening, walking jauntily past the Chinese not knowing she was there, hiding from him. She felt a cringe of shame. If only she had gone to the play. Andy would have understood. She could have written him a letter and explained. There was always another visiting day.

The notes of the young boy's recorder came into her head. She felt a burst of sadness for him and remembered the boy's father. Did he regret his outburst? Now, when he was back in his cell, when it was too late to say sorry? She pictured Andy's face, thinner, with a cut over his eye that he had dismissed. He was having trouble with an old solider along the way. Perhaps that's why he wanted the photos of himself in Iraq. A kind of boast.

How could she not have gone to see him?

On her way back to her room she saw that his room door was ajar and went in. She turned the light on. It seemed even colder in there and she pulled the sleeves of her dressing gown over her hands. The room looked exactly the same as it had the previous evening. Neat and tidy, nothing out of place.

It had been exactly the same when Andy was around. He hadn't been the untidy or lazy type. He hadn't lounged around his room all day, taking naps or listening to music. He'd got up early most mornings, a habit from being in the army, he had said. When she was lying in bed she often heard him moving around, tidying up. Going downstairs for breakfast she'd find him there, in the kitchen, organizing his breakfast things: a bowl of cereal, another plate which held a banana and an orange, with a small sharp knife on the side. He always had a smaller dish which held a number of vitamin tablets. The exact same meal every day.

He was strict in his habits. By eight-thirty he would be working, either in the garage or on the laptop or talking into his mobile. Sometimes Johnson would pick him up and he'd be out and away to some car auction. She never saw him slumped in a chair watching breakfast television. The army had been perfect for him. Its regimentation had suited him. Maybe prison was the same.

She walked across and opened his wardrobe. The blue shoebox that he'd mentioned was there. She sat cross-legged on the carpet and sorted through it. He'd said that the Iraq photos were probably at the top. She looked in a couple of packets but they were old snaps of the family, her gran, her mum, Andy and her. They were on holiday, on a day trip, on the beach at Colby East. She shoved them to the side. There were no pictures of soldiers in a desert.

She dug deeper into the box, pulling out some packets that looked older, one or two with elastic bands around them. They went back a few years and she smiled to see photos of Andy as a small boy standing in the garden next to Gran, a bike leaning up against his leg. Flicking through she saw other shots of her mum and Andy on the sea wall and for a moment she was struck at how young and pretty her mum looked. Her face was positively glowing, her smile wide and toothy, her hair blowing to one side in the breeze. There was also one of her and Andy standing together in the back garden. It must have been a family party of some sort because there were bits of other people at the edges. Andy was wearing jeans and a football shirt. He looked about thirteen. She was standing next to him, dressed up in dancing clothes. On her head she had the paste tiara that Gran had given her. It had always been too big for her and had to be fixed on with flat brown clips.

After looking at them all again she placed them back in the packet and then wondered what to do. The army photos weren't there.

She rubbed her hands together. The cold was making her fingers feel numb. She felt a yawn coming and stretched her arms up. Maybe she could slip into bed and drift back off to sleep.

A small stack of birthday cards caught her eye. She picked them up, surprised that Andy would keep such things. She fanned them out. There were five, and each one had a number on it. *Now You Are 8!*; *9 Years Old!*; *For Your 10th Birthday*; *11 Years of Age!*; *Now You Are 12!* She opened them and saw a line of handwriting in each. *From your dad*; *From your old dad*; *Love from Daddy*; *Best wishes from DAD!*; *Love Dad*. Inside one of them was a photograph of a man standing by a car. He was wearing jeans and a denim jacket and white boots. The name *Eddie Hanson* was written on the bottom in handwriting. He had a beard and shaggy hair and was smiling and giving the camera a thumbs up. She turned it over. *To my lovely boy, Andrew. Love Dad.*

She sat back, confused. This was her and Andy's dad. This smiling man dressed from head to toe in denim. She had pictured him as someone else entirely. She hadn't made that image up, she was sure. Sometime or other her mum had shown her a photo of this man that she had never met. She was sure that he'd been in a suit or more formal clothes with shorter hair. She hadn't been much interested at the time. Why should she? A man who lived somewhere else, possibly hundreds of miles away, who had no interest in their family. And yet he had sent Andy birthday cards. For five years after he left he had sent messages to his son.

But not to her.

She tidied the cards up and put them neatly in the bottom of the blue box. Then she stacked up the packets of photographs and lay them on top. It didn't matter. Eddie Hanson had left the house when she was a baby. She had no recollection of him. Why should she care if he had not contacted her? She put the lid on the box and tucked it back into the wardrobe. He had walked away, cutting the ties with his family, crisply, as if he'd used a pair of sharp scissors.

But not with his son.

After a while she forced herself to stand up and look around Andy's room. The photos of the soldiers must be somewhere else. She huffed. She couldn't be bothered to look for them now. She went back to her room. She didn't pause to take her dressing gown off but got straight into bed and pulled the duvet over her. She lay in the dark, trying to put the birthday cards out of her head. After a while of staring into the blackness of her room she sat up and put the light back on. She went quietly back into Andy's room and took out the blue box again.

She didn't go to school. All day she waited for a text or a call from Carl but there was nothing. She was perplexed. Had he not noticed that she wasn't in school? Didn't he want to ask her about the prison visit? Or tell her about the play?

Her mum came home from work just after eight. Elise had been watching out for her so the front door was open before she had a chance to knock.

"Hello, love. Are you feeling better?"

Her mum's cheeks were like two red apples and a small cloud of hot air came out when she spoke. She walked past as Elise mumbled a reply and peered out into the street for a few seconds, her eyes moving around, settling on Carl's front path. There was no one there, no sign of him, so she closed the front door.

"Mr Palmer said there's a job in the shop for you, remember, covering maternity for Sheila. Three nights a week, four till eight," her mum said, unwinding a long woolly scarf and unbuttoning her coat.

"Oh," she said.

"I thought you'd be pleased!"

"I am. I am."

She went back up to her room. Disappointment weighed her down. She sat on her bed and wondered what she was going to do next. She stared at the far wall where her bedroom adjoined Carl's. She had never been in there. She'd been in his house and his garden hundreds of times but she hadn't ever seen his room. She had no idea if it was pristine like Andy's or a mess. He'd been in her room, of course, on her sixteenth birthday, when they'd first kissed. That was just over a year before. They'd lay on the bed, him twisting and turning on top of her. Since then, whenever the kissing started, they always seemed to be standing up somewhere, her stretching up to reach him.

Unlike the scene she had witnessed on the night of the play. Carl and Sandy Miller standing face to face on the street. Sandy reaching out to touch him, her face level with his. Standing next to Carl she hadn't looked like a beanpole at all. They'd made a matching pair. There was nothing *passionate* about it and yet there was a connection between them, a spark of something. There was a sharpness about the two figures. In the murky fog of that evening they stood out, like models on a poster. It made her throat feel raw to think of it.

Was she was overreacting?

She'd been miserable after travelling all day and missing the trip to Norwich. She'd been stupid to stand back in the shop doorway. She should have gone up to the bus stop and waited openly. Then Carl would have seen her, come straight to her when he got off the bus. What was wrong with her? Why did she make everything so difficult for herself?

Like the birthday cards. She had gone back into Andy's room and looked at them again. Why couldn't she just have left them there and forgotten about them? Now it seemed as if they were stuck in her head. If Carl had rung she could have told him. He would have probably had a good explanation for them or made light of it. What did it really matter when it came down to it? Five cheap birthday cards. He would have made her feel better about it. She should have rung him and told him. It's what she would have done any other time.

She reached for her mobile and accessed his number. It rang a few times. The rings seemed loud in her ear, each one slightly longer and more impatient than the last. She wasn't going to leave a message. He would know she'd called, he would see her name on the screen of his phone. Possibly it would make him smile. Would it? She felt her arm beginning to sag and was about to cut the call when she heard his voice.

"Hi, Elly!"

"What you up to?" she said, lightly.

Her voice was casual. With her spare hand she was pulling the corner of her duvet into a point.

"Not much. Just packed a few things. I'm off to Dad's for half-term. Helping him do up an apartment in the city centre."

"That'll give you some Christmas money!" she said, her face dropping. He was going away.

"That's right. You feeling all right? Didn't see you at school."

"A bit under the weather. When's your dad picking you up?"

"In about an hour."

"Any chance of you popping in? There's just something I wanted to..."

"I can't, Elly. I've got something planned."

"Just for ten minutes. It's just something I found of Andy's. I wanted to show you..."

"Can it wait till I get back?"

"It'll only take five minutes."

"It's just that I'm really pushed for time. . ."

"Yes, sure. No problem. It can wait. It's not important. . ."

"Only I've got stuff to do."

"Hey, when you get back, we can do some more work in the café."

"That café. I've got a ton of splinters in my hands."

"Oh, and I thought of a new name for the company. *M and H Renovations*."

"The company?"

She gave a light laugh, her mouth as dry as sand. There was a gap before she heard his voice again.

"*The company*. Right! What you doing over half-term?"

"Some reading," she said, eyeing her books stacked in an untidy pile in the corner. "Got an essay to redo."

There was quiet. A number of things flew through her head that she wanted to say.

"I must go then, get packed," he said.

"All right. Send me a text."

"Will do."

The call ended before she could say another word. She kept her mobile tightly up to her ear. It was small and hard and cold but it had been full of life until the call ended, full of possibilities. Now Carl was gone and there were things she hadn't been able to say. It would be more than a week until she saw him again. There would be text messages, of course, but what good were they: wooden phrases, exclamation marks, abbrieviated speech? How could she express her emotions that way? She let her mobile slide down through her fingers and drop on to the bed. She closed her eyes tightly to stop the tears coming. Not just a week, eight or nine days. Working in Palmer's, being at home with her mum. Nothing to do, no one to see. It was a dark corridor of time that she had to get through until he returned.

A light knock on her room door startled her. She scrabbled round for a tissue. The door opened and her mum was there. She was holding a large brown envelope in her hand.

"You all right?"

She nodded, blowing her nose.

"I found those photos of Andy's. Just thought I'd let you know in case you were looking. I'll post them in the morning."

"OK," she said.

The Iraq photos. She had looked for them but had only come up with five old birthday cards.

A while later she was looking out of her mum's bedroom window, waiting for Carl's dad's car to pull up. She hadn't turned the light on, so it was possible to move the curtain to the side and look out without being seen. She was only there for a couple of minutes when some headlights came down the street. When the car stopped outside his house she realized that it wasn't Carl's dad's car. It was a silver car. The sight of it gave her a bad feeling. No one got out but she could hear the sound of music coming from deep inside, classical music.

She bent lower, trying to get a glimpse of who was in the car, but it was impossible. Then she heard Carl's front door slam. She expected to see him on his pathway but all she saw was a head of white hair illuminated by the street light.

Sandy Miller.

She watched, her hand gripping on to the curtain, as Sandy Miller walked down the path and without a backward glance got into the passenger seat of the waiting car. Then, as if the driver was making a getaway, the car raced off up the street.

Sandy Miller. In Carl's house.

She let the curtain drop and stood in the dark of her mum's room.

Later she went back into Andy's room and got out the blue box again.

THIRTEEN

November

Working at Palmer's gave Elise a good view of what was going on in the high street. At that very moment Carl Murdoch and Sandy Miller were standing with some other kids, talking and laughing about something. She took in every detail. The way that their shoulders seemed to touch. The fact that Sandy's pale complexion contrasted with Carl's black hair and honey-coloured skin. The way that she shoved him playfully and put her arm around his neck.

"Elise, I'm not paying you to stare out of the window," Mr Palmer said. "If there are no customers to serve, then you make yourself busy doing other things."

She nodded and began to straighten up the magazines on the rack behind her. She should be used to seeing the two of them together. They were always in the canteen at lunch time, in the library in free lessons, and they sat together in English. Outside school they could be seen walking on the street, idling in front of the chip shop, waiting at the bus turning-circle. A couple of times Elise had seen Sandy's white hair bobbing along the front garden path, going in or coming out of Carl's house.

It wouldn't last. Elise pulled a stool out and stood on it so that she could reach the magazines on the top. She tidied them and stepped back down. It would be over soon, she was sure. It was certainly more intense than any other thing that Carl had gotten into, but it would fizzle out. A few weeks at the most; then she would have Carl back again. She just had to keep her nerve. Pretend it didn't matter. Hold herself together.

Elise turned to find Mr Palmer standing behind her.

"Well done. That's the secret of success in this trade. There's always something to be done in a shop like this. My Rosemary says that I can turn my hand to anything. That's how I made it. Fancy a cup of tea?"

She nodded. When he walked off into the back of the shop she relaxed, letting her shoulders drop. She turned back to the window and saw that the small crowd of sixth-formers who had been across the street had gone.

It was four-thirty and it was almost dark. She could see some of the younger kids from school still walking along, their heads bent against the cold. They were heading for the chip shop. She suddenly fancied some chips. A small portion, in a cone, coated with salt and vinegar, so hot that they would burn her tongue. It wouldn't happen, though. She still had three and a half hours to do in the shop, listening to Mr Palmer's inane chatter. She slipped her free hand into her pocket and pulled out her mobile. She held it under the counter. It was on silent and she wanted to check if there were any messages, if Carl had answered the text she had sent earlier.

Saw you and Sandy getting off the Norwich bus yesterday. Did you have a good day? Elly

There was no answer. She sighed. Looking up, she saw Mr Palmer walking up the shop holding two mugs of tea.

It had been a week since Carl had first told her about him and Sandy. On the Monday after half-term Elise was sitting in the common room wondering where he was. She'd not seen him since he went to Norwich the previous Sunday. A beep told her she had a message. Holding her breath she read it through. *You won't believe this!* it had started. Carl and Sandy were together. It wasn't a surprise to her but still the words, coming from him, gave her an ache. She wrote her own message.

You and Sandy! Great! You make a good couple! Elly

How long it had taken her to compose it. How many times she had deleted the words and started again. How it pierced her when she received his immediate reply.

Thanks! I knew you'd be great about it. Carl

She sat hunched in the armchair and squeezed her mobile until her hand hurt. The door opened and made her sit up straight. Sandy and Gemma walked in. Sandy went to her locker but Gemma came and sat beside her. Elise managed a watery smile. She kept her eye on Sandy and laughed at some stupid thing that Gemma said. Sandy seemed to be reorganizing her stuff, holding a pile of books in the crook of her arm.

"That was a surprise, about Carl and Sandy," she said, in a low voice.

Gemma leaned towards her, holding one side of her bushy hair back. "Not to me, it wasn't. She's fancied him for a while. She confided in me. I told her he wasn't seeing anyone, so. . ."

Elise stared at Sandy. She felt an intense dislike for this girl.

After six there were more customers in the shop and the time went quickly. While Elise was counting out change to a woman in motorbike leathers she noticed Jason Bell come in. He took a basket from the pile at the front and then disappeared behind the shelves. A few moments later he reappeared with a single bottle of lemonade sliding about in the basket. He put it on the counter.

"This all?" she said.

"I've got something to mix with that," he said, in a low voice.

She shrugged and held the scanner up to the bar code on the bottle. He handed over a twenty-pound note.

"My brother's BMW is in the car park," he said.

"So?"

"So, we could go there. Later, when you've finished. I could wait for you. Have a few drinks."

She didn't answer. She put the twenty-pound note in the till, sliding it down behind the other notes. It was just after six-thirty. Soon she would be on her way home, back to her house, to spend another evening with her mum. She plucked out a ten-pound note and a five. She scooped up some coins. Jason's hand was open.

"Come on. We had a nice time a while back?"

"You didn't have to tell everyone about it."

"That was Todd, not me. I never said a word. I *wouldn't*."

She looked at him coldly as she placed his change in his hand. Just as she dropped the last coin, his other hand grasped hers.

"Come on," he said, his voice husky, "you can trust me. Todd's out tonight. He won't be coming back for the car."

She looked out of the shop window. The darkness was thick, the street lights pale and lemony. Ahead of her she had another evening without Carl.

"I'll meet you after work," he said, squeezing her hand.

"All right. I finish at eight. I'll meet you outside."

He was waiting for her when she walked out of the shop door, pulling her leather coat so that it wrapped tightly around her. She walked a step or so behind him. He turned to go down a side street but she pulled at his jacket.

"I want to go along the front."

"OK," he said, and walked, head down, towards the sea.

The gusts along the sea wall blew them to the side. Jason had his arm firmly around her shoulder. They were walking in step. At one point Elise laughed at their feet.

"We're like a couple of line dancers," she said, loudly, her voice rising above the wind and sound of the water crashing against the shore.

She looked up and saw the Beachcomber ahead. She faltered in her step for a second when she picked out strips of light along its side. Carl was in there. Part of her wanted to shake Jason off and go up to the door of the café and knock. It wouldn't seem so odd. It was what she'd been doing for the last couple of months. Why shouldn't she do it? She was Carl's friend, his helper, his pretend *business partner*. That shouldn't change because he had a girlfriend. Getting closer, she thought she could hear the faintest sound of music coming from the café. Was Carl in there alone? Or was he with Sandy? Either way she couldn't go in there. Not now.

Elise and Jason peeled off into the sand dunes, leaving the wind behind, weaving their way through to the car park. The BMW was there, parked at an angle. Jason got the keys out and unlocked the doors. She walked ahead, purposefully, and got into the back seat of the car. Jason followed her, fiddling about under the seat again and pulling out a new bottle of vodka.

"I got glasses this time!"

He pulled out a couple of plastic picnic glasses and poured vodka into each.

"Hold these," he said.

He opened the lemonade and poured it in. Elise drank some of hers, feeling the kick as it went down her throat. Jason drank his down all at once. Then he leant across to the front seat and put the keys into the ignition.

"What you doing?" she said.

"Putting the heater on and some music."

The car was instantly full of sound. The heater roared and in moments Elise could feel the hot air blowing from below her feet. Above it was a heavy beat, a song she liked. When Jason sat back he turned suddenly and kissed her on the mouth, his tongue pushing past her lips. He had his hand on her neck, stroking her skin, and the kiss seemed to go on and on and sent a tingle down to the pit of her stomach. When he stopped and leaned back she felt odd, her head a little dizzy. He was fiddling with something, his belt, unbuckling it, popping the button on his jeans, pulling the zip down.

"What you doing?" she said, draining the glass, putting it on the backrest.

"I really like you, Elly," he said, leaning back towards her.

She put her hands up and pulled his face towards her so that the kissing started again.

FOURTEEN

Carl and Sandy didn't last long. Elise heard about the break-up in the common room. The news perked her up. She decided to hang around in the hope that Gemma would come in and tell her the details. She passed the time looking at a poster on the wall for the Christmas concert. It was the same old stuff they had every year. *Music, Drama, Singing.* She had never taken part and never would. While she was reading it Sandy herself walked in and went to her locker. Her face looked pinched and her hair was not quite as springy as usual. Elise stepped across to her own locker, pulled it open and shuffled a few things about.

"Oh, Sandy," she said, as if something had just occurred to her, "when you see Carl, can you tell him I got another letter from Andy. There's some stuff in it about the jeep. . ."

"Carl and I had a falling out," Sandy said, blowing air between her teeth. "I may not see him before you do."

"Oh!" Elise said, her face full of concern.

"Yeah. These things happen. You know. . ."

Elise didn't know what to say. She really needed Gemma there as a middleman. Gemma usually managed to fill all the silences.

"You're his neighbour? Right? You've been friends a heck of a long time. Does Carl seem like the possessive type?"

"Not really. I couldn't say," she stuttered out; then, steeling herself, she said, "Why don't you come and sit down for five minutes. Tell me what happened."

Sandy seemed to deflate. She shut her locker and followed Elise. She knew that she should say something sympathetic. She'd never been that good in the company of girls, though. She had had friends but not really *close* friends, girls who would confide in her.

"I really like Carl. But he gets quite stressed about stuff."

"Really?" Elise said.

"It's really about Peter Fenner, you know?"

Elise frowned. Peter Fenner? She knew Peter. Hadn't they spent time together in the sand dunes on her sixteenth birthday? Now he was in her form group. He was an odd lad. He was into music and always had an iPod on, the earphones constantly stuck in his ears. Someone said he played guitar in a band with boys from St Benedict's. His appearance had changed in the last year or so. His hair was long and dark. His clothes were grey or black and he wore a calf-length leather coat that he said was second-hand, bought from a charity shop.

"He lives over my way? So we occasionally catch the bus together. And Carl sometimes walks me to the bus stop? When me and Peter get on the bus together he gets stressed and we have a row."

"He dumped you for getting on the bus with Peter?" Elise said, surprised.

"Not exactly, no. We just argued. You know, I really like him, but he can't tell me who I can and cannot get the bus with."

Elise nodded agreement. She pictured Peter at the bus stop wearing his long dark coat. Beside him was Sandy, with her long legs and white hair. She would have smiled at the mental image but Sandy's voice was scratchy. Elise hoped she wasn't going to cry. One thing was clear. They hadn't actually *finished*; they'd just had a row. She looked down at the file that Sandy had on her lap. On the front of it was her name and the name of the school, *Colby Academy of Modern Arts*. The handwriting was ornate, formed with a thin nib pen. The letters were tall and elegant, like Sandy herself. She didn't need to look at her own handwriting. She knew it was loose and untidy and some of it could be hard to read.

"Then there's the school concert. I'm going to play my violin and I know that Peter is going to play his guitar. Not together, you know, but we'll be at rehearsals and stuff. Of course I'll be friendly. I like to talk to lots of people. Carl can't change the way I am!"

"Why don't you just let him cool down a bit. He'll probably realize that he's been an idiot. Here, let's swap mobile numbers. We can keep in contact. I can let you know how he is."

"Would you?" Sandy said, taking Elise's hand and squeezing it.

"Sure," Elise said.

She gently pulled her hand back, embarrassed by the touch. She held her mobile out and took Sandy's. Elise scrolled down and then put her number on Sandy's phone. She took her own back when Sandy had finished. She was itching to go, to find Carl, to see what he had to say.

"See you later," she said. "I've got some work to do in the library."

Sandy gave a half smile, her fingers pulling at clumps of hair so that they hung over her eyes like tiny arrows.

Elise didn't go to the library. She took a walk round the school, looking in places where she thought Carl might be. She asked a couple of people and they said they hadn't seen him that day. Then she went home and sent Carl a text.

Where are you? Fancy a chat? Elly

There was no reply and she began to get agitated. She rang him but the call went straight to the answerphone. Maybe he didn't want to talk to anyone. She looked at the time. It was twenty past three and she was due at Palmer's at four. She put her coat on and headed for the Beachcomber.

It was a bright, cold afternoon. The sky was blue and she could see vapour trails criss-crossing it. She couldn't make out the aeroplanes; they were too far away, too small. The sea was flat and glassy and seemed to go on for ever. The air was still but she could feel its chill on her face. She rubbed her hands together and quickened her step until she reached the Beachcomber. When she got there she knocked on the door.

"Carl? You in there? Let us in, it's cold!"

There was no reply but she stood there for a moment. Was he there? Could she hear his breathing?

"Carl?" she said more softly.

She heard movement. When the door opened she smelled the heavy aroma of dope, sweet and sickly. He stood in front of her, a little unsteady on his feet, his eyes looking sullen and heavy. He was wearing his coat.

"What's up?" she said, following him inside.

It was dark and warm. She could hear the heater blowing hot air out. She clicked the light on but he shielded his eyes and waved his hand so she turned it off again. The café was semi-dark, some daylight coming through the gaps in the wood. He sat down heavily on the floor, his legs sprawled.

"Why are you smoking? I thought you said you wouldn't waste your money on that stuff?"

"Troubled times," he said.

"I heard you had a row with Sandy."

He shrugged his shoulders. She sat down beside him. The floor was hard and cold even though the heater was blowing at them.

"She seems upset," Elise said.

"I'm upset," he said, staring down at the floor.

"She says you were jealous of Peter?"

"Fenner?" he said, sighing. "I just think he's too friendly . . . or something. I don't know."

He was silent, his face in a frown.

"Oh, never mind," she said and put her arm round him. He slumped towards her. He felt heavy, as though he was going to fall off to sleep.

"Maybe she's not right for you," she said, her words slow, tentative.

"What? Did she say that?" he said, stiffening up.

She shook her head. Her hand was on his arm, rubbing circles on to his coat. He seemed to relax.

"Maybe you need a different sort of girlfriend."

He made a *hmph* sound. He seemed to be sliding down, his head moving from her shoulder to her chest.

"Someone..."

He nuzzled into her and she let her fingers comb through the back of his hair. *Someone more like me*, she wanted to say, but didn't dare. She moved his arm so that it lay comfortably across her. She felt his head on her chest and closed her eyes. The café was completely still, the light spearing through the cracks in the wood, the fire blowing hot air across them. She felt like drifting off to sleep, next to him, there on the floor of the Beachcomber.

"Stuff Fenner," he mumbled, moving about, as if he was going to get up.

She pulled herself into a sitting position and looked at her watch. It was twenty to four. She had to be at work soon. She didn't want to leave him but she had to make a move.

"I'm due at Palmer's. Why don't you get yourself

115

cleaned up and come round to my house just after eight? We could watch a DVD?"

He didn't answer. She stood up. She had to go. He looked like he was going to slump sideways again. He saw her concern and sat up straight.

"I'm all right, Elly. I'm going to go home in a minute. I'll sleep it off."

"See you later? Just after eight?"

He nodded.

She rushed home after she'd finished at Palmer's but he didn't come. She spent the evening looking out of the window, hoping she would see him walking up the path or along the street. She rang him three times but only got the answerphone.

Her mum went to bed early and at ten thirty she went into her room and got undressed. He wasn't coming. She had to accept it. She put on her pyjama bottoms and a strappy T-shirt. Then she pulled her dressing gown tight and went downstairs. She put the light on in the living room but it was too bright so she turned it off and put the side-table lamp on, leaving most of the room in shadow. She picked up the remote and flicked through the channels. The room was hot, like the rest of the house, so she shrugged the dressing gown off. After a few moments she lay on her side, her head on a small cushion. She watched the images flashing on the television screen, one music video after another. Her eyelids heavy, she dozed off.

Awhile later she opened her eyes to a knocking on the

window. She sat up instantly, blinking, staring round the room, wondering how long she'd been asleep. When the knocking sound came again she got up and stepped across to the glass. She pulled the curtain back. It was Carl. She looked at the clock. It was almost midnight. She'd been asleep for over an hour. She picked up the remote and pressed the mute button. Then she walked swiftly out into the hall. The lights upstairs were off and there was no sound from her mum's room.

She opened the front door. Carl was leaning against one side of the porch.

"Hi!" he said, his eyes dropping down, looking at her bare shoulders and tight top.

"Ssh..." she said, putting her finger over her lips, "Mum's asleep. Come in."

She pulled his arm so that he was in the hallway. She closed the front door quietly. She gave him a little push in the direction of the living room. He was jerky, unstable. When they were in the front room and she had shut the door she smelled the alcohol.

"I thought you were going to go home and have a sleep."

"I did. I had a few cans first. Then I remembered I said I'd come round. Saw your light on."

"Sit down," she said.

He began to move about, struggling to take his jacket off.

"Hot in here," he mumbled.

"Here," she said, "I'll help."

He was floppy. She manoeuvred his arm out of his jacket and then pulled at the other one. She lay it on the other chair and then sat beside him, her knees up under her. For once she was taller than he was.

"How many cans did you have?" she said.

He didn't answer. He pushed his head into her arm and murmured something. She could feel his hot breath on her skin. She was aware suddenly of her bare arms, her neck and chest. She was only covered by a thin T-shirt.

"Did you go and see Sandy?" she said.

He shook his head and she felt a tiny spark of hope inside. She turned and lowered her head to face him. His eyes were open but sleepy.

"Is it over?" she said, wanting him to talk, wanting him to confide in her. Like they'd done for years. Best friends.

He shrugged. His eyes flicked down to her chest and back up to her face. She could feel his hand holding her arm, his grip tightening. She was close to him. She could smell the alcohol, she could feel the heat of him, she could sense his chest rising and falling with each breath.

"What's the matter?" she said, her voice low.

"Elly. . ." he started.

She leant forward and kissed him. Softly on the mouth. His head slid back along the seat so that he was half lying down. He wove his hands through her arms so that he was encircling her, pulling her with him so that they were both lying side by side on the settee. She put her arms up so that they were round his neck, flattening herself into him. The light from the television flicked across them.

During the kissing she felt herself turning so that she was on her back. He seemed awake suddenly and was lying on top of her, his kisses coming one after the other, his fingers under the straps of her top, his hand moving up and down her body. After a moment he paused and pulled something out of his pocket. It was a condom packet. His eyelids were heavy but he had a sheepish smile on his lips.

"I haven't done this before," he said, his words slurring. "You'll have to show me what to do."

She pulled him towards her, kissing him, holding him as tight as she could. She'd never done it before either but she didn't say it.

FIFTEEN

The next morning she stood tall and looked into the mirror. What she saw pleased her for once. She was in proportion. Her hair looked thick today, her skin creamy. She went closer to the glass. Her lips were puffy, darker in colour. As if all that kissing had changed the shape of her mouth. She liked the way it looked. She stepped back. She'd put on a deep pink jumper over the top of her skinny blue jeans. Underneath she had on some new high-heeled boots that she'd bought. The total effect was to make her look *much* taller. She turned sideways. Her breasts stood out but in a good way. She placed the palms of her hands across her chest and felt a faint tingle there. She closed her eyes, remembering the night before.

Out of the blue it came, the thing she had wanted more than anything. Her and Carl together. She'd been patient. She'd waited for this thing to finish between him and Sandy. She'd been there in the background; quiet, unassuming, undemanding Elly.

Afterwards they'd both lay sleepily on the sofa, side by side, the television flashing silent pictures across them. Carl went very still, and that was when she'd realized he was asleep. He had to go home. They couldn't be found like that in the morning by her mum. She'd stood up, pulled her dressing gown on and shook him, telling him he had to go. He'd half-walked, half-stumbled out of the door into the freezing cold night, making footsteps on the frosty path. She'd closed the door. She felt so full of emotion she thought she might sing out.

Now she pulled herself together. She should go to school. She'd left it later than her usual start. She wanted Carl to go ahead of her, to get into school early. She wanted him to be sitting in the common room wondering where she was.

She picked up her bag and made sure she had the right books. She took her mobile off charge and saw with surprise that she had a text. It had come earlier that morning. She grinned. It was most likely something from Carl. Probably wondering where she was, why she wasn't at school. But the name *Sandy* appeared and she felt indignant for a moment, as if Sandy was in some way intruding on her. Then she remembered that she'd given her number to her and asked her to get in touch.

Hi Elise! Did you see your next-door neighbour, Carl? How is he? I really miss him. Sandy

Too late, she thought. Sandy was just too late. She put her mobile in her bag and walked out of her room. The house was quiet; the only sound was the thrum of the central heating. She walked into the living room. She'd tidied it the night before after Carl left. There was no sign of anything that had happened there. It was neat; even the scatter cushions were lined up.

She left the house. The streets were empty and she walked jauntily, taking big breaths as she went along. She felt full up with something: delight, satisfaction, joy. It was cold but there was no wind, so for once her hair hung loosely instead of flying all over the place. She turned into the high road and walked into Palmer's to buy something. Her mum served her.

"You're in a good mood today!" she said.

Closer to school she heard a beep. Pulling her mobile out, she saw she had another message from Sandy.

You know Carl better than I do. Do you think I should say sorry? Sandy

She put her mobile on silent, Sandy's words taking a tiny bite out of her feeling of well-being. She would be upset when she found out about them but that was how it had to be. It wasn't her fault or Carl's. When she got to school she went straight to the common room. It was a few minutes until the bell for recess.

The room was half empty but up at the far end she could see Carl talking to a couple of other kids. He looked round and she gave him a nod. She sat down in a chair and waited for him to come over. She opened a book and stared down at the page. She felt him move in her direction, his footsteps on the floor, his voice coming closer, the chair beside her groaning as he sat in it. She finally looked up, her finger on one of the lines on the page.

"What you up to?" he said.

"Working on my *Death of a Salesman* essay."

She turned to face him. She wanted everything to seem normal. As though their being together was a natural thing. Carl and Elise, finally a couple. He was leaning forward in the chair, looking tense. He had his elbows on his thighs and the tips of his fingers were touching off each other.

"Have you done the essay?" she said.

She felt her mobile vibrate in her pocket. She took it out and glanced at the screen. The words *Sandy Calling* were there. She wasn't going to answer it. She turned it over and lay it on her lap. She didn't want Sandy interrupting her talk with Carl.

"Who's that?" he said.

"No one," she said.

He looked away. *He's embarrassed*, she thought. *He feels awkward*. If only she could put her hand out to him, touch his face, something *physical* to take away these first few moments of uneasiness. Seeing her in public after such a *private* act. He was uncomfortable. She could understand that.

"How's your head?" she said, remembering his slurred voice from the night before.

"I had too much to drink last night. On top of the smoke..."

He shook his head, his eyes on the floor. The bell went for change of lessons and he looked up over to the door. She could see he was edgy. On top of everything else, he thought Sandy was going to come in and find them together. He probably didn't want any upset.

"Last night. . ." she started.

"Are you all right? After last night? I was worried that you. . ." he interrupted, a frown wavering across his forehead.

"I'm great," she said, leaning towards him, her voice dropping to a whisper. "You know me. I take everything in my stride."

She wanted to reassure him. She didn't want him to fret about her. She didn't regret what she had done; she wasn't embarrassed. She was *proud* of it. He shook his head, his eyes straying towards the door as it opened and groups of sixth-formers came in. She didn't quite know what he wanted to hear. She looked down at her mobile lying in her lap. She touched it with her fingers. She knew what she *wanted* to say to him. How amazing it had been. How she had wanted it to happen for so long. Ever since that first birthday kiss.

"Had any letters from Andy?"

He was making conversation to break the tension. That was OK. Why not? Eventually they would get over the awkwardness.

"About a week ago. They've moved him to a nearby prison."

"Good."

"Oh, I've got something for you!" she said.

She rummaged in her bag. She wanted to lighten things up a bit, make Carl feel more relaxed. She leant forward to get to the very bottom of her bag and her mobile slid off her lap and bounced on to the floor, rolling towards Carl. He picked it up.

"I bought these at *great* expense."

She talked on as she searched her bag. She was waffling, she knew, but she kept going.

"Here!" she said, holding out the tube of sweets.

Carl didn't look up. He was staring at the screen on her phone, his face screwed up, his mouth twisted.

"Is that Sandy's message you're looking at? I was going to read it myself in a minute. . ."

But he was scrolling down. She knew that he was reading the other messages. She should have been annoyed that he was looking at her phone but it wasn't unusual for them to play around with each other's mobiles.

"So, here is your present. Don't say I never buy you anything!"

She leaned across, offering the sweets.

"Those texts came this morning," she said, clearing her throat. "Here, take your wine gums."

She held the packet in mid-air, her eyes taking in Carl's expression; his eyes, moving back and forth across the words on the tiny screen. He was taking a long time reading the messages. She gave a little laugh but he didn't look up.

"I have to go," he said, giving her back her mobile, standing up.

"Shall I come?" she said, puzzled.

He shook his head. He picked his bag up, his face blank, unreadable. Had she said something wrong?

"I'll catch you later," he said.

He strode off across the room and went out of the door. She sat stiffly on the chair, the tube of sweets lying in her hand. Something was wrong. She picked up her mobile and looked at the open text on the screen. *I miss him.*

She knew then what had happened. He had gone to find Sandy.

After school she took over from her mum in Palmer's. She sat down at the till and worked her way through a basket of shopping. The customer, a young woman with a ring through her bottom lip, was sorting through the cards in her wallet, taking them out, looking at them, slotting them back in. In the end she paid for her shopping with a twenty-pound note. Elise counted out her change and then looked back into the shop, where her mum was supposed to be picking up some stuff for their tea. Instead she was standing talking to Mr Palmer. They were by the soft drinks and crisps and her mum was bending her head back to look up at Mr Palmer. Elise wondered how her mum didn't get bored with the man, having him breathing down her neck all day.

The green telephone began to ring and she hesitated. Was she supposed to pick it up? Mr Palmer was already walking towards her, though. Once at the counter he snatched up the receiver. She turned her face away, towards the window, as she heard him talking to his wife.

Carl and Sandy walked past the shop.

She stared at them through the glass. They were on the

opposite pavement, walking closely together. In the back of her head she could hear Mr Palmer's voice. *Of course I will, Rosemary. Wafer-thin ham and a carton of coleslaw. I'll bring them up presently.* Carl and Sandy were almost the same height. A handsome couple. They contrasted each other, Sandy with her white hair and pale skin up against Carl's dark hair and satin-brown complexion. They weren't holding hands or touching but there was no gap between them. Carl was saying something, his face turned towards her, his lips moving.

Elise slipped out from behind the till. Mr Palmer had replaced the receiver and was talking quietly to her mum: *Rosemary can't eat wheat, you see; it upsets her.* She left his voice behind, walking as close to the glass as she could get, watching them as they made their way up the high street towards the bus stop. A little further up, when she could only see their backs, she saw Carl's arm raise up and drape itself across Sandy's shoulder. Then they merged into one figure.

She dropped back and stood by the shop door, her legs feeling weak and her head pounding. She didn't feel well.

"Bye, love," her mum said, going out the door into the street.

It was twenty-five past four. She had three and a half hours to go until she could go home and bury herself under her duvet.

SIXTEEN

Elise stayed in bed for the weekend. When it came to Monday she didn't get up to go to school. She simply couldn't edge the duvet off and slide out of the warmth. The clock radio was playing and a song came on that she liked. Normally it would have made her move, hum along, but today it sounded worn-out, as if she'd heard it too many times. She reached out and pressed the button and the radio went silent.

She felt unwell. She couldn't imagine herself getting up. She pushed her face against the cool part of her pillow and tried to picture herself walking through the grey town. Her head would be angled into the cold, her hands deep in her pockets, her bag pulling one shoulder down. She'd pass Palmer's and the bus turning-circle and walk along the lanes by Marsh Park. She would have to side-step the younger kids in their dark uniforms. They would never hurry but simply stroll along in twos or threes or fours, their arms linked, chattering or singing or laughing. She would stride out and leave them behind. At school she would go to the sixth-form common room and sit in one of her usual seats. After a while the door would open and one of them would come in; Sandy or Carl. She would have to smile, to look pleased to see them when all the time her insides were breaking apart.

She rolled over and closed her eyes. There would be no school.

She *was* physically unwell. She had headaches and tiredness. Sometimes her chest felt heavy and there was pressure on her temples, her eyes feeling as though they would pop out. When that happened, she closed the curtains in her room and lay on her bed in the pink haze of her bedside lamp. When she got up she went back into the living room but felt cold even though the central heating was sauna-like. At night she woke up sweating, her sheets damp.

Her mum made her go to the health centre. The doctor she saw had her notes halfway out of the pouch, his pen poised and ready to write something down. When she described how she felt he sighed, slid her notes away and said she probably had a virus. He told her to take paracetamol and plenty of fluids and rest. It would go in its own time.

Carl and Jason sent her a few texts and she got a couple of calls from Gemma, who wondered where she was and what was wrong. Carl came by once, bringing her some work for her English class. He stood beyond the doorstep and handed her the papers, saying he was in a rush. She watched him go and felt a yawning hole inside her.

Her mum did extra shifts at Palmer's and came home one day with a bag full of remedies: Lucozade, Olbas Oil, honey, oranges, painkillers, vitamin C. She also brought a box of chocolates from Mr Palmer, who said they missed her in the shop.

"Do you think," her mum said, unpacking a carrier bag, "that this – the way you're feeling – that it could have anything to do with Gran?"

"Gran?" Elise said.

"It's a year next week."

"Oh."

A year since Gran died. Elise hadn't registered the time, the month, the date.

"I just thought. . . I know you and your gran were thick as thieves."

"I'm just not well, Mum. I don't think it's anything to do with Gran."

"Being a year – it's sort of significant. A whole year without her."

Elise nodded. Her mum shrugged.

"Gran wouldn't have wanted us to cry all over again," she said.

"No."

"I didn't remind Andy. I thought he had enough on his plate."

"Yes."

The days slid by. The weekend passed. She was no longer ill but she wasn't well either.

Wednesday was the anniversary. Elise felt restless and went out into the town. She waited until mid-morning to avoid seeing anyone from school. She sat on the sea wall, braving the bitterly cold air, and looked out at the water. It was low tide and the wet sand was as smooth as cement. It reminded her of a time when she was a child, six or seven, and she'd had mild chickenpox. She had to stay off school for three weeks even though she only had a few spots and felt well. Her mum had been at work and she'd been looked after by her gran. They'd spent some time on the beach, away from people, collecting shells, exploring, playing I Spy, printing words on the wet sand with their footprints. *We'll write our names*, Gran had said. It was easy for Elise. She spelled out the letters with short heavy steps, ELLY. For Gran it had taken longer. Gran wanted to write her stage name, MARILYN. Her real name was Mary, but Gran said that had been too plain for show business.

What would Gran have said about Carl and Sandy? She would have had an opinion, Elise knew that.

When it started to spit with rain she walked home along the sea wall, turning her face away from the Beachcomber and making her way through the dunes. There was no BMW parked in the car park, just an old white van. In daylight the place looked squalid. The white lines of the parking bays had faded and the tarmac was pitted with holes. A carrier bag had caught on to a nail halfway up a telegraph post and was flapping like a flag at half mast.

At home she wandered from room to room. She walked in and out of her mum's bedroom, the back dining room and the living room. She began to see her gran everywhere. In the dining room her china filled the French dresser. A lavish set of dishes which lined the shelves; plates with frilled edges, cups with scalloped handles, bowls that were edged in gold. There was a shelf of novelty cups that she had collected in her days of dancing. *Look at these, my petal*, she'd said when Elise was little. And she had lined them up and counted them and sorted them into colour and size and eventually put them back in the dresser.

In the living room was Gran's special picture. A big frame in the centre that held a photograph of Gran when she was performing in the End of the Pier show at Great Yarmouth. At the bottom, in the right-hand corner, Gran had autographed it *With love, Marilyn*. Elise ran her finger across the glass where the signature was.

In her mum's bedroom were some of Gran's clothes. Elise pulled out a hanger that was covered in a plastic bag. She lay it on the bed and gently rolled the plastic bag up until the dress underneath was revealed. It was a shiny blue fabric. It felt like silk but it wasn't; rayon or satin maybe. The top of the dress was tightly fitted with small seams like arrows which puffed out the breast section and then narrowed down to a tiny waist. It wouldn't have fitted her or her mum. The skirt flared out and fell below the knees. On Elise it would have come down to her ankles.

She rolled the plastic down again and replaced the dress in the wardrobe, where it joined several other outfits. They hung in a row, the plastic loose and filmy, floating on the hangers; ghostly reminders of her gran.

A year before, on her way to school, she'd gone into the living room to say goodbye. Gran had been sitting in her armchair across from the television. She was wearing a turquoise tracksuit with furry slippers and white socks. The television was on, the volume louder than necessary.

"You off, Elly?" her gran said, raising her voice above the sound.

"Yep," she said, staring at her gran's head. It was covered in white heated rollers. Every section of her hair had been divided up and curled around the hot metal prongs. Elise knew it took her ages to do and then, in five or ten minutes, she would take them out and have a head of curly hair.

"Here's a bit of pocket money," her gran said, pushing her hand down the side of the cushion and producing a bulging purse.

"Thanks, Gran!"

Just then she heard Andy's voice calling from the hallway.

"Want a lift, sis?"

"Yes, please!" she shouted, raising her voice.

"Here you are," her gran said, holding a five-pound note out. "Is that Andy?"

An advert came on to the telly. It had a cartoon Father Christmas and reindeers on it and there was a jaunty song with the sound of musical bells ringing. It was deafening.

"Come on, Elly; I said I'd meet Johnson in ten minutes."

"Thanks, Gran," Elly said, plucking the note from her hand and moving away, towards the door.

"Don't I get a kiss? You kids, always in a hurry. Is that Andy rushing off as well?"

"Bye," Elise said, ducking back into the room and giving her gran a peck on her powdery cheek.

Andy came into the room, a heavy bunch of keys jangling impatiently.

"How come she gets money and I don't? It's discrimination."

"You can have some. . ."

But Andy stopped her talking by bending down and giving her a loud smacking kiss on the lips.

"Bye, Gran," he said, moving past Elise and walking out of the house.

Elise pulled the front door shut as she ran after him. Making her way to Andy's car, she glanced sideways in the hope that Carl might come out and share the lift but there was no sign of him. When Andy dropped her off at the school gates he said, *Don't I get a kiss?* in a silly high voice and she told him to get lost and walked off towards the common room.

At just after two, as she and Carl were walking back towards school after lunch, Andy's car pulled up alongside them. He pushed open the passenger door and told her to get in.

Her gran had died that morning.

*

134

The day after the anniversary her mum seemed concerned.

"When do you think you'll go back to school? You've been off nearly two weeks. Got to go back some time! What about your coursework?"

Elise nodded, but an idea was growing inside her. Did she need to go back to school at all? What if she just left? Just stopped going?

The thought frightened her and excited her at the same time. What a gesture it would be. To announce that she didn't need school, didn't care for studying any more, wasn't bothered about seeing any of them again; Carl, Gemma, Jason, Sandy. It made her feel reckless for a few hours, heady, as if she'd solved some great problem in her life. She got up on Friday morning feeling full of energy. She would tell her mum at the weekend. She would make her see that staying on wasn't what she wanted. She already had GCSEs and AS-levels. She could start earning money. Why not?

The post arrived. She picked up the letters and saw that one was for her. She recognized Sandy's handwriting immediately, the long loops and the neat slant of each word. She thought it might be a get-well card. She opened it sluggishly and was faced with the American flag, red, white and blue. The colours were loud and there was glitter stuck to the stars. The card seemed to light up the hallway as she took it out of the envelope. On the inside she was surprised to see the words, *Please come and celebrate Sandy's seventeenth birthday at 8 o'clock on Friday*

5th December. It wasn't a get-well card. On top of the printed words was a Post-It. *Sorry you're sick. Hope you make the party! Sandy.* At the bottom was a row of Xs.

She was instantly annoyed by it. Sandy had only been in school for five minutes and now she was throwing a party. Everybody would be impressed all over again, swooning over this American girl. She went into the living room and tossed the card on the chair. She sat down, smouldering. She picked up the remote then she put it back down again. She crossed her arms and looked round the room. She stopped when she got to her gran's picture. The words *With love, Marilyn* stared out at her. Her real name was Mary but that was too ordinary so she made up a new one. *I had to toughen up, I had to look after myself!*

Gran wouldn't have let this bother her.

On the day Gran died it was her mum who found her. It was just after eleven and Gran was still sitting on the armchair. It was over two hours since Elise and Andy had left. She hadn't moved. Her big chunky purse was still lying on her lap. She was sitting upright, her head leaning on one of the wings of the chair, her heated rollers still in place.

A massive stroke, the doctor had said. Her mum told her that he'd clicked his fingers when he said it. As if it had been instant. A second, no more. She was alive. Then she was dead. Elise had never understood the suddenness of this. Surely, she'd thought, the body needed a little time to wind down. The heartbeats would become less frequent, the blood flow would slow, breath would stay in the lungs a little longer. Then the light would fade in the eyes until it was just darkness.

But Gran died in an instant.

When Elise and Andy arrived home Gran's body wasn't there. She had already been taken away by the undertakers.

Her mum was sitting in the kitchen bent over the table, her head in her hands, rocking back and forth. Andy went and sat beside her, put his arm around her. Elise couldn't move. There on the table lay the heated rollers, lined up in a row.

Her mum must have unrolled the hair, each curler individually. Maybe she even brushed it. That's what Elise would have done.

"Anything you want me to bring back from the shop?"

Her mum's voice broke into her thoughts.

She came into the living room and picked up the card that was lying on the chair.

"A party invite! That's nice! Do you think you'll be well enough to go?"

"Yes," Elise said, quietly, looking up at her gran's picture.

Maybe she should go back to school after all.

SEVENTEEN

December

Elise slipped into her Monday-morning English lesson later than everyone else. The other kids appeared to be making notes from the text so she sat down and got her books out and started to flick through the pages until she got to the right section. She opened her diary and her notebook and took the lid off her pen. She felt strange, being back in school after so long at home. She fixed her hair behind her ears and straightened her skirt so that it didn't get wrinkled at the back.

The teacher, Miss Peacock, came over to her.

"Are you feeling better, Elise?" she said.

Elise nodded. Her eyes were drawn to the silver rings that sat on each finger of the teacher's hands. Like knuckledusters.

"You got the work I sent home?"

"Yes, miss. I've done a lot of it."

"Good. You can't afford to miss such a lot of time at this stage in the course."

When she went back to her desk Elise looked around at the rest of the group. They were sitting on three sides of a square. Carl was across the way from her and caught her eye immediately. She gave him a smile. Sandy was next to him, writing something down. Beside her was Gemma, looking down at what Sandy was writing, then making notes herself. Further round was Peter Fenner, scanning the text for something, his finger moving up and down the page. She could see the white flex of his earphones mingled in with his jet-black hair. Further round was Jason.

Miss Peacock had taken her reading glasses off and they were hanging down on a chain.

"What does this play tell us about fathers and sons?"

There was a few moments' silence. Peter Fenner started to speak.

"That sons don't have to be a replica of their father? No, *replica* is a bad word. . ."

A couple of girls sniggered at this. Elise took a deep breath. Peter continued to talk about fathers and sons. She thought of her own *father*. Edward Hanson. *Eddie* Hanson. *Ed* Hanson. The birthday cards came back into her mind. She'd not looked at them for a while. *To my lovely boy, Andrew. Love Dad.* She wondered what sort of memories Andy had of him, whether he had pined for him. She suddenly wondered whether, in fact, Andy had had *contact* with him in the years after he left. Had he picked Andy up on Sunday afternoons and taken him out, to Norwich maybe, to the cinema and a McDonald's? Had Andy got dressed neatly and waited by the window for him to drive up while she toddled around the room, oblivious of her father's lack of interest in her? Her gran had called him a *useless article*. When she was small she had had no idea what that meant. Her gran had called him a lot of other things as well and her mum had always shushed her. It didn't matter. Elise had never had a moment's interest in him. He was a man from the past; a missing person that she hadn't wanted to find. She wondered what Andy felt about him now. She glanced down at her diary and saw the prison visit written in red for later that week. Her mum was going on her own. She said that Elly wasn't physically up to it and that she'd already missed too much school. And the new prison was only an hour away so the journey would be easy. It had given her a moment's anguish but she was also relieved. Seeing Andy and knowing about the birthday cards would make her feel weird. He'd phoned at the weekend and she felt awkward and hadn't known what to say to him. In the end she'd asked him about the appeal and he told her that a preliminary court date had been set for the first week of January. *Who knows, you might see me sooner than you think!* he'd said. She wondered if she would ever mention Edward Hanson to him.

The sound of Carl's voice made her tune back in to the discussion.

"Is it that a dad should allow his son to do what he wants to do?"

Miss Peacock didn't give her opinion. She was twiddling the rings on one hand, looking around the room. Elise knew that this awkward silence would prompt more answers. It was Sandy who finally spoke.

"Is it that a father shouldn't try to live his life through

140

his sons? Or get them to try and achieve the things that he hasn't been able to achieve. Like, he's living a kind of vicarious life?"

Miss Peacock gave a contented smile.

"Very good point, Sandy. Now, let's look at an early scene between Willie Loman and his two sons."

There was a general groan and the sound of pages flicking. Gemma was nudging Sandy in admiration. Elise picked up her pen and began to make notes. After the lesson people came up to her, asking her how she was feeling. Jason Bell was one of them.

"Glad you're back," he said, walking along the corridor with her. "You coming to Sandy's party? It'll be a laugh!"

"Maybe, I don't know," she said.

She headed for the library to be on her own. Sitting down at a computer, she logged on and looked at her school email box. There were dozens of emails. Most of them had to do with work she had to give in, targets and pastoral information. There was also a reminder from the careers teacher to complete her form for university, as well as an email from Sandy about her party. It had been sent to everyone who had received an invitation.

Don't forget to party at Sandy's! Friday at eight. Don't be late!

She pressed the delete button.

At lunch time she went to the refectory. She sat in the sixth-form and staff area, which was cordoned off from the rest of the school. She bought some pasta and found a table away from the teachers. Just as she began to eat,

Sandy appeared holding a carton of drink and a banana. She came straight across and sat down opposite her.

"Hi, Elly! You're looking well!"

"Thanks."

"Glad I've caught you. You must have had an awful time. I wanted to come round and visit but Carl said you were better left alone. He was probably right. I had mono – I think you call it, like, glandular fever? – when I was a kid and I was so ill? It took me six months to recover."

Elise nodded and took a forkful of pasta and chewed it quickly.

"Anyway, I wanted to thank you for the peace-making you did..."

Elise frowned. Sandy was looking straight at her, face to face. She was too close. There didn't seem any *room* between them. Sandy was pulling the skin from the banana strip by strip. Then she lay the pieces carefully on the table. Elise ate more of her food, wondering how quickly she could get away. She edged back in her seat and looked across the barriers at kids from the rest of the school. They were sitting in rows chatting, laughing, nudging each other, shouting. How carefree they seemed.

"When me and Carl split?" Sandy said, taking a bite and chewing. "He told me you showed him those texts I sent? He said it was only then he realized how upset I was. I'm so grateful. Otherwise we might never have got together again. He's stubborn. I'm stubborn. Who knows what would have happened?"

Elise nodded. Her pasta seemed to have no taste. She chewed for a few moments and then managed to swallow. There was still a bowlful in front of her but she didn't know if she could manage it.

"We should be friends, you and me," Sandy said.

Elise put her fork down.

"We've got this big thing in common!" Sandy said. "We're both close to the same guy. You're Carl's friend and I'm his girlfriend."

"I must go," Elise said, standing up, "I have to see a couple of teachers."

"What about your food?"

"I'm not that hungry," she said, picking the dish up and turning away.

"I'll catch you later." She could hear Sandy's voice from behind. "And don't forget the party on Friday!"

EIGHTEEN

It was impossible to keep away from Sandy.

She was always in the common room showing off her violin, talking about the Christmas concert. Or Elise bumped into her in the corridor and had to stop for a two-minute chat about nothing. Or she was hanging round outside school or in the town with Carl. She was even in most of Elise's classes. There was no way of avoiding her.

In history, Mr Packer asked the class to get into groups of three to discuss the causes of the English Civil War. There was an odd number, and Elise and Peter Fenner ended up as a pair. Peter put his leather coat over a spare chair and sat on the other side of Elise's table. Moments later the door opened and Sandy came into the room puffing, as though she'd run all the way from the other end of the school. She said *sorry* a number of times and Mr Packer pointed a finger in the direction of Elise and Peter. Sandy rushed over, her pale skin flushed. She pulled another chair across and squeezed in on the edge of them. She spent a breathless minute looking round and getting her stuff out of her bag.

"You guys don't mind if I join you?" she whispered.

Peter shook his head and Elise gave a stiff smile and picked up the handout and began to read it through. Peter explained to Sandy what it was they had to do.

It was a small table with barely enough room for the three of them to lean and write, so Elise didn't bother. She sat back and let the other two do the work. She gazed around the class. Everyone was so busy, so involved. Why did she not feel like that? Why wasn't she writing notes and planning answers and discussing points? She looked at Sandy and Peter, their faces in profile, listening to each other, making suggestions, asking questions. The whole room seemed to be full of animated voices. It was like some odd soundtrack that she wasn't part of. It made her think again about the vague plan she had come up with when she was off sick about not coming back to school. Maybe she would still do it. She could give it to the end of the week, until Sandy's party. Then she would make a decision.

Each group had to give a short feedback. Sandy and Peter took turns. Elise sat quietly, colouring in the Os on her handout, thinking about what sort of a job she could realistically get with her qualifications. When the bell sounded they all packed up and Elise got out of the room before the others.

In the common room she found some girls to sit with and half listened to their conversation as she drank a carton of juice. She looked down at her black trousers. She'd bought them the previous weekend. She also had her new high-heeled boots on underneath. They looked good together.

"Are you going to Sandy's party?" one of the girls said.

"Not sure," Elise answered.

The conversation continued as Elise crushed up her empty juice carton. She collected her things together, got her media textbook out of her locker and walked towards the door. Just as she was about to leave, she heard Sandy call her name. She rolled her eyes and held the door partly open.

"Elly, are you going to your form room before lunch? Can you give this to Peter? I picked it up by mistake in history."

"Sure."

Elise took a notebook off Sandy. It had the words *Peter Fenner* written on the front, above a stuck-on picture of an odd-looking band. Elise recognized them. They all had jet-black hair and wore flowing cape-type coats. It explained Peter's new look.

She walked towards the media rooms. After the lesson was over she packed up her stuff and was last to leave the classroom. She stood in the corridor wondering which way to go: the refectory? Common room? Library? After a few moments' indecision she headed for the school gates and home. She had a key skills class after lunch but it wouldn't hurt to miss it. She could put it down to her ill health. No one would ask; probably no one would actually *notice*.

Walking up her street, she saw Carl coming out of his house. He grinned and it gave her a little flip in her chest. Even now, after everything that had happened, he had this effect on her. She walked tall, her boots scraping the pavement, and met him outside her gate. He looked sleepy, as if he'd only just got out of bed. His hair was sticking out at the side and she wanted to reach over and smooth it down.

"Are you off to school?" she said.

"Unless I can find something better to do. Hey, you look different, nice. . ."

"Oh, thanks very much. Meaning I usually look awful."

"No!"

"Come in for a drink," she said. "You won't miss much at school."

He hesitated for a single second. She had meant that he wouldn't miss much in the way of lessons but maybe his thoughts had gone immediately to Sandy.

"Why not."

She put the kettle on for herself and poured him a Coke from the fridge. She'd dropped her school bag on the table and some of her things had slid out. She scooped them into a pile. Carl sat down.

"Mum's seeing Andy this week. Is there anything you want to tell him about the jeep?"

"Nah, nothing to report. I've hardly had any free time to work on it since half-term. Now that I've finished at the Beachcomber I need to get some work that pays money. My dad's offered me some stuff over Christmas but I need some now. Everything *costs* so much. And with Christmas coming up and Sandy's birthday on Friday . . . I'm just broke."

"What about your mum?"

"Not worth the ten-minute lecture I would have to listen to."

He sat down at the table, moving her books out of his way, drinking down half the glass of Coke in one go.

"Is it Sandy? Is that why you're so broke?"

He shook his head. "We don't spend anything. I just go round her house. She's got this gazebo in her garden that's got heating and furniture and stuff. We spend a lot of time there, watching DVDs, listening to music. We get chauffeured round anywhere we want to go."

"She's got a *chauffeur*?" Elise said, startled. "I knew she was well off but I didn't. . ."

"No, her *mum* drives us around."

Elise smiled at her mistake.

"I'll have to ask Dad for an advance."

"*Advance*? What are you, an *American*?"

"A loan, then," he said, sheepishly.

"You'll be talking about *cell phones* next."

"What's this?" Carl said, looking at the pile of books on the table.

"Don't change the subject!"

He flicked through the pages of her history notebook.

"Let me see, *The English Civil War was inevitable. Discuss.*"

"Don't read any of what I've written!"

She plucked her book from his hand. He looked at the pile again and picked up Peter Fenner's notebook.

"How come you got this?"

"Sandy asked me to give it to him," she said, tutting. She'd forgotten all about it. It would have to wait until tomorrow.

"How come Sandy had it?" Carl said, puzzled, flicking through the book.

She shrugged. It was too much bother to explain, that and the fact that she wanted to steer the conversation away from Sandy.

"Look at this!" he said, a note of annoyance in his voice.

She looked at the page. She recognized some notes from the discussion that morning, a list of causes of the Civil War. Beside them Peter had written the word *Sandy* and underlined it a couple of times. It was probably when they were feeding back to the class. So what?

"Why's he written her name? Three times! Look! What's her name doing in his book? I don't get it."

Carl looked like he was getting upset. Over what? His girlfriend's name written in someone's book? She felt herself becoming irritated. She was hot so she unbuttoned her cardigan. She held the corners of it out and shook them, letting some air get to her chest.

"Maybe *I'll* give it back to him!" Carl said.

"No, I will," she said, reaching across the table and taking the book out of Carl's hands.

Carl glared at her, his eyes dropping after a few seconds. His lips were tightly closed, his forehead in a frown.

"Why are you like this about Peter Fenner?" she said, her voice steady.

"He's always hanging around Sandy."

"He lives in her village. They're in some of the same classes. They're bound to know each other."

"He's always there, talking to her about books or essays. Or asking her about the USA."

He eased his chair back as if he was going to stand up.

"He's a friend, that's all."

"In any case," he went on, "he's probably better suited to her than me. He's going to go to uni, so is she. His parents are well-off, so are hers. They're the same type."

"Hardly!"

"Then there's the Christmas concert. *Peter's so good on the guitar*," he mimicked in an American accent. "You've only got to look at the two of them," he went on, "Peter and Sandy. They go well together."

She was amazed that Carl should feel like that. Whenever she looked at Sandy and Carl they seemed perfect for each other. Her with her white hair and pale skin; him with his dark skin and black hair. The same height, the same build. The same attractive looks. They just *went* together. And then she wondered: was he talking about *colour*?

"You mean because they're both white?" she suddenly said.

He was startled. He shook his head. "No, I didn't mean that," he said.

She looked at his dark eyes and his sepia skin. She loved his colour.

"It's nothing to do with colour," he said. "Why do you

150

say that? Do you think it's something to do with colour?"

"No, I just thought that's what you meant."

"Has someone said that?"

"No!"

"I didn't mean *colour*. He's just more her *type*."

"But she's mad about *you*."

"She doesn't always seem so pleased to see me."

"Because you're giving her a hard time. You have to trust her."

"I do trust her."

"She trusts you. The situation's not so different. He lives near her and I live near you. She trusts *you*."

"Why shouldn't she trust me?" he said, "I mean... She has no reason..."

He stuttered for a moment. She watched him closely. Maybe he'd just remembered the night they'd spent on the sofa. The night when they lay side by side. While Sandy was sending conciliatory texts, Elise had been kissing him until her lips were sore.

"Sandy does trust me. She trusts me completely," he said, looking away, not meeting her eyes.

It took a few moments for her to work out what he meant. Then she understood, and a thin pain seemed to pierce her chest. Sandy trusted him because she viewed Elise as no threat to her whatsoever. Elise wasn't a potential partner for Carl in the way that Peter might be for Sandy. Elise was no one, a neighbour, a short, heavy girl who was good for passing messages on. She lay Peter's notebook down on the table in between them.

"Sandy just asked me to give this to him. I wish I'd never mentioned it!"

"But why did she have Peter's book in the first place?"

She could have explained. She could have told Carl that the three of them were working as a group and that he and Sandy were working out which point they would each talk about. She could have described how they were crushed round one desk and Peter's book had got mixed up with Sandy's things. That would have made Carl feel better. But why bother? She stood up, took her half-full cup of tea to the sink and poured it away.

"I don't know," she said.

Why should she explain?

That evening, in Palmer's, Elise spent most of her time reorganizing some shelves at the back of the shop. It was busy and she was constantly moving out of the way so that customers could get by. It was mindless work but she was active and she liked being out of Mr Palmer's eye. The time went quickly. Just as she finished the shelves she heard footsteps up the tiny aisle. It was Gemma, her hair blown here and there by the wind. She was wearing a jumper and jeans but no jacket. She was shivering, the sleeves of the jumper pulled down over her hands.

"Carl and Sandy had this big row in front of everyone."

"How come?"

"He's started on at her. He's got this thing about her and Peter."

Elise thought of the notebook, still in her bag, ready to return the next day.

"Have they split up?" she said, using a mildly uninterested voice.

"Hope not. What with the party on Friday. Are you coming?"

"Yeah," she said, "I think I will come."

"Good. Now, what was it I came in here for? Oh yeah, pasta sauce. One of those'll do!"

She took a jar off the shelf that Elise had just been working on and walked off towards the till. Elise watched her big hair bobbing up and down. She hadn't been out for ages. Why not go to the party?

NINETEEN

Her mum was due back from the prison visit in the afternoon. Elise, on her way home from school, decided to wait for her at the bus turning-circle. It was just after three-thirty. The sky was streaked with orange where the late-afternoon sun had emerged from the clouds. There were kids from school all over town: some hanging around in groups, some waiting for the bus, some outside Palmer's, others further up, sitting on the sea wall even though it was fiercely cold. Her mum got off as a line of year sevens pushed and jostled to get on to it. Her skin was pink with the heat of the bus and she was smiling. She made a shivery face as soon as she stepped into the cold.

"Andy sends his love," she said, taking Elise's arm and walking along beside her. "He's doing really well. He's got a couple of mates on his wing, one lad from the forces. And he's got a date for his appeal hearing. January 8th. Oh, he told me to give some cash to young Carl for working on the jeep."

She talked on as they walked and Elise's spirits rose. January 8th wasn't far off. He was probably counting the weeks. And the money for Carl would be a bonus. He could do more work on the jeep and she'd see him on his own more.

"I'll just pop in and see Mr Palmer," her mum said as they were coming up to the shop, "see how Rosemary is. She took a bad turn last night."

Elise nodded. She stood in one place and looked up and down the road in case Carl appeared. She was keen to tell him about the money but there was no sign of him. She'd left him at school, sitting in the common room talking to Sandy, who was waiting to take part in a concert rehearsal. She exhaled, rubbing her hands together, feeling the cold soaking into her. Parked further up, she noticed Todd Bell's BMW. Todd was sitting in the driver's seat, the passenger door hanging open, music spilling out on to the cold street. On the pavement were a small group of year-eleven boys. It wasn't an unusual sight, Todd Bell, in his car, at the end of a school day. Some of the kids from school hung around with him thinking they were rubbing shoulders with the town gangster.

She looked into the shop and saw Mr Palmer and her mum talking. He was probably giving her mum chapter and verse about how sick his wife Rosemary was. Her mum was nodding sympathetically, acting as though she was his best friend, not an employee. She was about to go in and drag her mum out when she saw Penny Murdoch, Carl's mum, turning on to the high street. She was walking briskly towards her, her breath making small clouds.

"Hi, Elly," Penny said, when she got up to her. "Mum all right?"

"She's in the shop," she said. "Where you off to?"

"Carl left his mobile at home. I said I'd walk round with it. I expected to see him somewhere, here."

"He's at school, I've left him there twenty minutes ago."

"Oh, well. I'll walk it. Do me good. I could do with the exercise!"

"Shall I come? Keep you company?" Elise said, perking up. She had no particular place that she had to be.

"That'd be nice," Penny said.

Elise dashed into Palmer's to tell her mum. She caught up with Penny a few metres on.

"What do you make of this Sandra Miller?" Penny said.

For a moment Elise had to think. Sandra. Sandy.

"She's all right."

"I like her. You can't help but like her. But Carl's only seventeen. It's all getting too serious too quickly. It's *Sandy says this, Sandy says that*... It's causing a few rows at home."

They walked away from the shops, towards the road that led to the edge of the town. Elise didn't know what to say. She just ummed when Penny went on to tell her about the difficulties she'd been having with Carl. She wanted him to finish the university application forms and he'd refused. There was no point, he'd said; he had no intention of going to uni. She'd driven him over to Norwich and had a raging row with his dad. Now no one was talking to anyone.

But that wasn't the worst.

Elise pulled her coat around her. Up ahead was Marsh Park. She could just make out the sign that said, *No Bicycles: No Skateboards: No Roller Skates.*

"He's now told me that he might spend next summer in Connecticut. Staying with Sandy and her family. He may go back to the USA with them in June and stay until September, when she goes to college."

Elise went quicker to keep up. Carl in America?

"I like this girl. Her family sound nice. But really, what future is there in it?"

Elise didn't know how to answer her.

"You know what, Elly? I always thought he'd get together with you. He said as much himself. When was it? Just months ago, maybe at the end of the summer. We were just chatting and we got on to talking about me and Michael and what went wrong in our marriage." She paused for a moment. "I said something to him like, Oh, me and your dad, we met and fell in love in four weeks, we were married in three months and you were born the following year. That was the trouble. If we'd known each other longer. If we'd been friends, like you and Elly, for example, I said. He told me he'd thought about you and him getting together. Being such good friends and all, but he said that you weren't ready. You still had an eye for other lads. I said to him, You can't blame Elly. She's too young to get serious with anyone."

They were passing Marsh Park. Elly glanced in. There was no lighting, just the last wash of daylight that showed the swings and flower beds and the grass. Beyond it was Marsh Wood, like a dark wall at the edge of the park. No one was in there. The park was in twilight, mist already forming on the grass. *He told me he'd thought about you and him getting together.* The words ran through Elise's head again and again. Penny was walking ahead and Elly followed a couple of steps behind. They continued on in the direction of the school. Cars edged past them on the lane, their headlights stretching out into the brown night. Elise pushed her hands into her pockets as far down as they would go. *He might spend next summer in Connecticut.* In her head she saw Carl on an American beach, the sun shining down, the sand white, the sea cobalt blue.

"Has he said anything to you about this America trip?" Penny said.

Elise shook her head. Why would he talk to her about it?

"You know what my big worry is?" Penny said, as they rounded a bend in the road and saw up ahead the yellow lights of the school buildings.

Elise mumbled, "What?"

"That he'll go to Connecticut with Sandy and never come back."

A cold, blank feeling took hold of her. Carl leaving Colby East. She might never see him again.

They were at the school gates. The building was lit up and looked warm in the darkening countryside. There were still teachers' cars parked in the car park and in the distance, over by the playing fields, Elise could see the white sports shirts of boys on their way back from football training. Tiny figures who dashed through the darkening night. Above them the floodlights of the playing fields turned the mist an eerie yellow.

"Don't tell Carl I said this, but you know what I wish for?" Penny said. "I wish that they'd have a big row and finish. She can go back to the States and Carl will stay here. How mean of me!"

"I did hear that they had an argument yesterday..." Elise said, her voice crackly.

Just then, Carl emerged from the main entrance of the school.

"Hi, Mum! Got my mobile?" Carl called, looking quizzically at Elly.

"Here." Penny handed over the mobile as Carl leaned over and gave her a kiss on the cheek.

"Hi, Elly, what you up to?"

"Just chatting with Penny."

"Come in, Mum, see ten minutes of the rehearsal. Sandy's playing. She'd be so chuffed if you watched. You too, Elly."

"Oh," Penny said, "OK."

"I've got to shoot off, actually," Elly said, turning to go, taking a couple of paces to distance herself. "My mum's expecting me."

"Thanks for keeping me company," Penny called.

"Coming to the party tomorrow?" Carl shouted.

"Probably," she said.

She quickened her step, her head down, her shoulders tight. She walked back on to the lane and through the mist, keeping to the edge so that cars could nudge past. She passed by Marsh Park and only then did she let herself loosen up, glad to be away from Penny and Carl and Sandy with her violin. Eventually she turned into the high street and saw the sign for Palmer's up ahead.

Carl had wanted her. All those weeks, months – years, even – that she had wanted him and he hadn't a clue. She'd let the moment pass and now he had someone else. It was her stupid fault. Carl thought that she didn't want to get serious, that she still had an eye for other lads. If only he had known the truth. If only she had told him. Now it was too late.

When she got to Palmer's she went in to see if her mum was still there. She nodded distractedly at Maureen on the till, who was scanning packets of sweets for a couple of year sevens. She looked around. Her mum and Mr Palmer were nowhere to be seen.

"Mr Palmer and your mum are making tea," Maureen said.

Elise nodded and walked down the aisle towards the door that was marked *Private*.

What was it that Penny had said? *I wish that they'd have a big row and finish. She can go back to the States and Carl will stay here.* Then Sandra Miller would be history.

She pushed at the door to the kitchen. It didn't open. She pushed it again. It seemed stuck.

"Mum?" she called.

There was a noise from behind the door. Movement.

Elise's head was bursting with Sandy. This tall, thin girl with her white-blonde hair and her effervescent smile. This girl who had wandered into her life and taken something precious from her. Elise *hated* this girl.

"Mum, the door's stuck!" she shouted, rattling the handle.

There was the sound of keys turning. The door opened slightly and then further again, and her mum stood there. She was pulling her coat on, trying to straighten the collar, which was sticking up.

"Sorry, Elly, I must have turned the key by accident. I don't know why I did that."

Mr Palmer was behind her, smiling in a sickly way at Elise.

"Are you ready to go?" Elise snapped, turning away from the tiny kitchen, pointing herself towards the door, trying to draw her mum along in her wake.

"Coming," her mum said.

Elise strode up the aisle to the exit. She let herself out of the shop and walked a couple of paces, stopping for a second to let her mum catch up. Penny's words kept coming back to her: *He'll go to Connecticut with Sandy and never come back.*

Maybe she could stop it. She could work out a way to set them against each other. Make them argue. If she could deliberately split them up. Then he wouldn't go to America.

He would stay in Colby East with her.

TWENTY

The party started at eight but Elise didn't get there until after ten. The bus dropped her off at Little Cumber, a village on the way to Walcott, and she walked a couple of hundred metres off the village green and found the house. It was more modern than she'd expected, double-fronted, with a gate at the side that presumably led to the back garden. The windows downstairs were full of light and there was the sound of music in the distance, as if the party was out the back of the house. She unbuttoned her coat, straightened the black top she was wearing and pushed the front door open.

A woman looked round as soon as she entered the house. She was tall, with long white-blonde hair held back off her face by a black Alice band. There was no doubting that it was Mrs Miller, Sandy's mother. She was wearing a long linen dress that was criss-crossed with wrinkles. Round her neck was a giant set of amber beads and on one hand a matching amber ring

"Hi," she said brightly, opening her mouth to show brilliant white teeth. "Coats upstairs, straight ahead, room at the back of the house. Food in the kitchen, drinks and music in the conservatory."

The upstairs room at the back of the house turned out to be Sandy's bedroom. Elise lay her coat on top of a pile and looked round. It was old-fashioned. A giant wooden wardrobe sat on one side of a double bed, taking up most of the wall. The bed had some kind of silky duvet, most of which was covered by coats. At the headboard was a row of tiny sequinned cushions. By the window was a hall stand. Instead of holding coats, Sandy had hung clothes there, nighties and floppy scarves with fringes that looked like they had come from a second-hand market. It was arty.

She stood in front of the mirror that was on the door of the wardrobe. Reaching into her jeans pocket she pulled out a lipstick. She applied it carefully and pursed her lips together. The deep red colour made her skin look white. She liked it. Behind her, reflected in the mirror, was Sandy's bed. For a second she imagined Sandy and Carl lying there, side by side, the silky duvet covering them. A feeling of envy coiled its way inside her. She put the flat of her hands across her midriff and held tightly, as though it was a physical pain. Noise from downstairs broke into her thoughts. She pulled her eyes away from the mirror, put her lipstick in her pocket and headed for the party.

The kitchen was full of adults. There was a mumble of conversation, a few raised voices and ripples of laughter.

"Elly! At last!"

Sandy appeared. She had tight black trousers and pumps on. Over the top was a short sequinned blouse. Her hair looked stiffer, as if she'd had it done at a salon, and there was a single pink stripe through the front. She gave Elise a hug as if they were the oldest of friends and pulled her through the kitchen into the conservatory.

"OK, so there's music here," Sandy said, "drinks over there. No smoking in the house but it's OK to do it in the garden. The gazebo is open. Great top! Look, Gemma, here's Elly!"

Sandy took her across to the drinks table and left her with Gemma. After a few moments' idle chat she looked around. The conservatory was as big as the ground floor of Elise's house. It had cane furniture and a terracotta floor. The music came from a small CD player but the sound came out of tiny black speakers placed all around. In all there were about twenty-plus kids from school, some she knew better than others. Jason was sitting down and she gave him a nod, managing to ignore Sue Perkins, who was sitting at his side. Carl was across the room with Sandy talking to some other kids. Sandy's sparkly top seemed to light up the corner where they were standing. Elise gave Carl a little wave. Then she went to the drinks table and picked up a can of beer. She glanced across the room and was momentarily taken aback to see Peter Fenner on the other side of the conservatory, by the CD player, talking to a couple of other lads. She hadn't expected to see him there. She looked back at Carl. His arm was around Sandy's shoulder, his fingers stroking the top of her arm. Elise held her breath and watched as he whispered something in Sandy's ear and she turned and kissed him on the mouth.

It didn't look as though he was worried by Peter Fenner.

She wished she hadn't come. She took a drink from her can of lager and felt it bubble down her throat. It was Sandy's party, Sandy's house, her friends, her food and drink. Maybe this wasn't the place to try and change things. Maybe she should just have a few drinks, then go home. Monday was a new day. It would be easier to make things happen in school, when Carl and Sandy weren't always together.

But she was here now and it would look stupid if she suddenly turned tail and went home. Pulling herself together, she walked across to where Peter Fenner was and sat down on the seat beside him.

"What you up to?" she said.

"Just looking through the music," he said.

He was quite good-looking in an odd way. His hair was too long but he had a nice face. He was wearing a white T-shirt with the name of a band scrawled across it in black. He must have noticed her looking because he began to straighten it, his fingers covering the band name.

"That band is so last year," Elise said.

"I like their music," he said.

"I like their music, but the T-shirt is so *last year*."

"And your clothes? Are they this year?" Peter said.

"What's wrong with them?" she said.

"Actually," Peter said, "nothing's wrong. I like what you're wearing. You look different lately," he said, turning to her and looking down at her blouse, his eyes lingering on her chest.

She was reminded suddenly of the day at the beach when they'd gone into sand dunes and she'd let him touch her. She'd been getting back at Carl but it hadn't been an unpleasant experience. He'd been nervous, she remembered, his fingers inexperienced. He'd kissed her with great force for a while until she'd pulled him back and showed him how to do it in a different way.

"You look funereal," he said.

She spluttered. "What does that mean?"

"It means that you always look as if you're about to go to a funeral. Wearing black all the time. You didn't always dress like that."

"So?" she said.

"I think it looks good. All you need is some sunglasses and you'll look like a French film star! Even your name sounds French."

She was taken aback. She had some put-down ready to hand but she felt strange at what he'd said. Like a *French film star*! It made her smile. He kept talking for a while, asking her about herself. She told him about Andy in prison and about her job in Palmer's. He told her about his record decks and the band he was in with the St Benedict's boys. They talked until Sandy burst over and asked for a change to the music and pulled Elise and Gemma up to dance with her.

After the dancing she looked round and saw that Peter was talking to some other kids. She walked around by herself. Someone had got the dance lights going and the conservatory was full of bright colours coming on and off to the beat of the music. Every now and again there was strobe lighting and everything that was white shone out before turning pink and blue and yellow again. She had a couple more drinks, a few dances, and talked to some other people. The music slowed down and Jason appeared and persuaded her to dance. Looking to the side, out into the garden, she saw some lads sitting on the steps of the gazebo opposite. Some were just smoking cigarettes. A couple were passing dope along. Carl was on the end, drinking from a can.

It meant that Sandy was on her own for once. When the track stopped and Jason went off, she headed towards her, stretching up to talk into her ear, her voice rising above the music.

"Sandy. Would you do something for me?"

"Sure."

"I really like Peter. Could you tell him that for me? Only most people don't take me that seriously but I think he's nice."

Sandy looked surprised. She looked over to where Peter Fenner was talking to some other kids.

"Why don't you tell him?" she said. "He'd like it better it if came from you!"

"I'm too embarrassed. Anyway, I'm always joking with him. He wouldn't believe me. Could you tell him when he's on his own? Away from other people? That way he won't think I'm having him on."

"Is this an example of British reserve?" Sandy said, shaking her head and smiling.

Elise nodded. "I'd be really grateful!"

"OK, it'd be good for you to have a guy. And Peter's so sweet!"

"Don't talk to him straight away. It'll look too obvious. Let me get out of the way, then tell him."

Sandy nodded in a motherly way and Elise walked off out of the conservatory into the garden. She rubbed her arms with the cold. She headed for Carl and sat down beside him. The wood beneath her had a dampish feel but she stayed where she was. The conservatory was lit up like a stage.

"Andy's got some money for you, for working on the jeep," she said. "Come round some time and I'll get it for you."

Carl nodded in an absent-minded way.

"Sandy looks nice," Elise said, looking at the sparkling top through the conservatory windows. "She always looks so glamorous. She could be a model."

She said *model* but the word *dancer* came into her head.

"She wants to be a teacher," Carl said, his words a little slurred.

Sandy's legs were long and the sparkles on her top and her white-and-pink hair gave her a glitzy look, as if she were in show business. Resentment bubbled inside Elise.

"I was surprised to see Peter Fenner here," she said. "I thought you were hacked off with him."

As if by magic, at that very moment, Sandy moved across the conservatory to where Peter was standing. Elise edged to the side so that she could see clearly. Peter turned to Sandy, his white T-shirt changing colour with the flashing lights.

She glanced sideways at Carl. He was looking straight into the conservatory. Whether he was registering his girlfriend talking to Peter she couldn't tell. She looked back. Sandy had done as she was asked. She'd moved Peter into a corner away from other people. They were standing close and she was talking into his ear. No doubt the music was too loud for her to do it any differently. The lighting was too indistinct to see the expression on Peter's face but their bodies were close.

"You don't have to worry," she said, quietly, in Carl's ear, "Sandy's just giving him a message from me."

Carl didn't answer. He looked up, more focused now on what was happening.

"I was a bit dismissive the other day," she said, her voice light, "when you were talking about Peter Fenner and Sandy, but, you know, I really do see what you mean. They look sort of *right* together."

Just then the strobe lighting came on and Peter's white T-shirt glowed, as did some of the sparkle of Sandy's top. It was as though the two of them were the starring couple in a musical. Elise felt Carl stiffen beside her.

"But it's definitely not about colour. The fact that he's white and you're black isn't important for Sandy."

"Mixed race," he said, quietly.

"I meant that."

She could feel Carl sitting absolutely still. In the conservatory, Sandy had her hand on Peter's arm.

"She's taking her time giving him my message!"

Elise kept her eyes forward. Peter was laughing at something.

"I've got this *thing* for Peter," she said. "You know he's in a band? I don't know if I've got a chance, though. Between you and me I think he only has eyes for one person."

Carl was losing his grip on his can of beer. It dropped on to the grass. Then he stood up and walked away, towards the conservatory. Elise sat very still and watched as he went inside and walked straight through the dancers and headed for the corner that Sandy and Peter were standing in. She tensed for a moment. Carl wasn't going to *hit* Peter? But Carl simply stood tall, his legs apart, his shoulders sticking out. As if he was strutting. With one arm he hooked Sandy away and pulled her across to another part of the room. Then they both stood face to face. Sandy had her hands on her hips and Carl's face was like thunder.

It was time for her to leave. Her head down, she walked through the kitchen and into the hallway. Jason was there with another lad.

"We're going back to Colby. Want a lift? My brother's coming."

"OK," Elise said, "I'll just be a minute."

In the bedroom she found her coat. She picked it up and was about to leave when her eye settled on the things that were hanging on the ornate stand. She picked off a white nightie with lace around the top. It looked old-fashioned, like something in a Victorian museum. Underneath it, hanging on another hook, were two silky vests. She picked one of them off. It was pink, with brown lace around the neck and armholes. It was pretty. It was small. She looked at the label. It said *Bloomingdale's*. It wasn't a make she knew. No doubt it was the kind of thing Sandy wore underneath her outer clothes. It wasn't like she needed a bra. Unlike Elise, who needed a substantial bra bought from a chain store in Norwich. Her underwear was practical, not stylish. She unhooked the second vest. It was identical but the colour was a darker pink. From downstairs she heard her name being called. She replaced the deep pink vest and was about to put the other one back when she hesitated, stroking the fabric with her fingers. It only took a moment to fold it over a couple of times and put in her coat pocket. Then she replaced the white nightie and left the room.

She sat in the back of the taxi with Jason on one side and another lad on the other. In the front was Sue Perkins. Todd Bell had loud music on and the car raced through the country lanes, skimming the overhanging branches as it went by. After a few minutes' driving she felt Jason's arm slip round her shoulder.

"Come back to mine," Jason whispered. "I'll get rid of the others."

She let her head lay back on the seat. She was tired but

she felt comfortable and happy. Why not go back to his house? She'd made a good start tonight. Next week she would carry it on. It would take time, months maybe, but she would break them up. Then Sandy would go home to America alone and she would still have Carl.

TWENTY-ONE

The party was the main topic of conversation in the sixth-form common room. There was gossip about drunkenness, drugs, sex and rows. Gemma told Elise about Carl and Sandy falling out and then making up. *Everyone's used to their little rows by now!* Gemma had said. When Sandy came into the common room she was laden with a school bag, an instrument case and a sports bag. After putting most of it in her locker, she came over to where Elise was sitting.

"Any word from Peter?" she said in a half whisper.

Elise shook her head, adopting a glum expression. She'd been surprised that Peter Fenner hadn't called her the previous day. After talking at Sandy's party she thought he might have been interested. He wasn't exactly in demand, with his floppy hair and his silly long coat.

"Maybe he's just shy," Sandy said.

"Gemma told me you and Carl had a falling out over Peter. I feel like it was my fault," Elise said.

A flicker of annoyance crossed Sandy's face. It was an expression Elise hadn't seen before.

"Carl has some *issues*."

"Thing is," Elise said, taking a breath, looking round

the common room, aware of the number of kids that were arriving, "I know Carl really well. And I know what he's like with girls." She paused. "I really shouldn't be telling you this..."

"What?" Sandy said, "Go on, I won't say a word."

"I hate to see him throw something important away."

"What?" Sandy's voice dropped to a whisper.

"I've seen him with girls. There's never been anyone that's lasted," Elise said, the truth coming easily. "He just loses interest."

Sandy sat up straight, her mouth slightly open.

"He used to say that those girls were so... What was the word? *Weak*. The minute he got together with them, their personalities seemed to disappear."

Sandy leaned forward.

"I shouldn't be saying this."

"I won't say a word to him. I appreciate what you're telling me."

"I think – and I could be wrong – I think the reason he's stayed with you is that you have this strong character. You won't change everything to please him. This thing with Peter is an example. Carl wants you to avoid him but the fact that you won't shows what a strong person you are. I actually think that's the thing that attracts him to you."

Sandy looked thoughtful. "I am a strong person."

"He loves that. You're a challenge for Carl. That's why he likes you so much."

Sandy nodded, a far-away look in her eyes.

"This jealousy thing. It's what keeps Carl interested."

The common room was filling up. All the chairs were taken and the noise level had risen. Elise could hear the distant sounds of music coming from a number of nearby iPods.

"I was going to try and distance myself from Peter. You know, just to make things easier," Sandy said.

"It's up to you," Elise said, "but, in the long run, it might have the opposite effect."

"You could be right."

Elise noticed Gemma at her locker, and at that moment Peter Fenner came into the common room. She knew Sandy was looking at her so she looked down at her lap, as if she were embarrassed.

"Peter's just not interested in me," she said.

"I'll speak to him," Sandy said. "He'll be at the rehearsal for the school concert tonight. It's over by seven and I'll have a chance to talk to him then."

"Don't say anything in front of other people. I'm not *desperate*," Elise said.

"Trust me. My mom can't pick me up so I'll be taking the bus. We're the only two who go that way."

Elise stood up. "Thanks. I really appreciate it."

She walked across the room, giving Gemma a smile as she went. Peter had his back to her so she went past without a word. Just as she reached for the door it swung open and Carl stood there.

"Hi, Elly!" he said, happily.

She opened her mouth to reply to him but he sidestepped her and headed off towards Sandy. She turned round and watched as he sat down beside her. Their faces were in profile, looking at each other, each starting to speak as the other did. She found herself staring at them. Around her people fussed at their lockers but she couldn't get going.

"You all right?" a voice said.

Jason Bell was beside her. She nodded up at him.

"I was going to give you a call," he said, taking her elbow and moving her out of the door, into the corridor.

"Right," she said.

"Come round my house after school. We could listen to some music?"

"I can't make tonight," she said. "Tomorrow?"

"Done," he said.

He walked off up the corridor towards his class. She watched him for a moment. There was a swagger about him, as if he'd just achieved a gold medal by arranging something with her.

After school she got changed. Pulling out a clean jumper, she came across the silk vest that she had taken from Sandy's bedroom. It gave her a moment's consternation. She took it out and held it up to the ceiling light. The brown lace was more of a coffee colour and made the pink look light, almost white. It wasn't just a vest, she now saw; it had darts which shaped the breast area like a loose bra. It was sweet and pretty. It filled her with envy. She shouldn't have taken it. She wasn't a *thief*. She didn't want any of Sandy's *things*. She just wanted Carl back.

Irritated, she tossed it on to the bed.

About five, she picked up an envelope with £100 in it from her mum's dresser and went next door to Carl's house.

"I've got this money for you, from Andy," she said, holding the envelope up.

"Come in. Mum's still at work," he said, smiling.

She followed him to the kitchen.

"How is Andy? I never got a chance to ask you."

She sat down at the kitchen table while he put the kettle on. She told him about the appeal date and what her mum had said about how the new prison was better and how Andy had made a friend.

"Eighth of January. That's really good."

"If the sentence is reduced he could be home within weeks," she said, pushing the envelope towards him on the table.

"He needn't have bothered with the money. I've not done much on the jeep lately," Carl said.

"That's why he asked Mum to give it to you. He's hoping that most of the body work will be finished by the time he comes out. He wants you to look on it as a sort of job."

"I'll be able to do a bit more this week. Sandy's going to be at the concert rehearsals. Next week, though, I'm staying at Dad's. He's got a big job at this house in Norwich. A new extension that they want decorated in time for Christmas. There's a big bonus if we get it done so I'm missing the last few days of school. It's not like we do much then anyway."

"You'll miss the concert."

"I'll survive!" he said, pouring boiling water into two mugs.

His mocking tone cheered her up. She knew how Sandy went on and on about the concert. It was as if she was playing at the Albert Hall. He placed a mug of tea in front of her and she was quiet for a moment and then she spoke.

"The thing about Sandy..."

"What?"

"Oh no, never mind."

"What about Sandy?"

"It's not my place to say."

He was quiet for a moment and sipped his drink. She opened her mouth, as if she was going to say something, then shut it again.

"What?" he said, his face in a grin.

"It's just that you two, you know, you seem to get on so well."

"Yeah."

"I think she feels worn down by this jealousy stuff."

He was looking down at the table, twisting his cup around.

"Anyway," she went on, "I had a chat with her, tried to smooth it out."

Carl looked uneasy. He had both hands round his mug, hugging it. She wanted to reach across to him, to grab one of his hands and hold it. Instead she sipped her tea.

"You'll lose her if you carry on. And face it, she could have anyone she wanted. Anyone."

Carl exhaled loudly.

"That's just my opinion. You can ignore it."

Elise pushed her mug away and then got up. She walked out into the hall and Carl followed her.

"Don't say anything to her tonight. It'll look too obvious. As if I've been talking to you."

"Tonight?"

"When you meet her?"

"I'm not meeting her tonight. She's got a rehearsal."

"Oh, I thought..."

"What? Did Sandy say she was seeing me?"

"No, maybe not. I just thought I heard her say something about meeting up afterwards, at the bus stop."

"Most probably it was her mum. You know, her *chauffeur*," he said, smiling.

"Why wouldn't she pick her up at school, though? Oh well, I probably got the wrong end of the stick. I should go."

She went back into her own house. At six-forty she walked into her mum's bedroom and stood by the window. She was holding the silk vest, rubbing the fabric between her finger and thumb. After a short while she heard the sound of Carl's front door shutting. She looked out of the window and saw him walking swiftly up the road.

He had gone to see who Sandy was meeting.

She folded the vest up carefully and tucked it back into her drawer. She waited about ten minutes; then she put her coat on and went out and headed for the high street. There was a strong smell of frying so she went into the chip shop and bought a cone of chips. The television was on, showing a football match. The lad who served her was from school and she chatted to him while putting salt and vinegar on her chips. She stood watching the match, keeping half an eye on the street, picking out one chip after the other.

At twenty past seven Carl passed the chip-shop window, heading back towards home. She dashed out after him. She had to speed up.

"Carl!" she called, catching up with him, holding her chips out. "I had a yearning for some chips. Want one?"

He shook his head.

"What you up to?" she said.

"Nothing," he said, without looking at her.

"Nothing?"

He didn't answer.

"Hey, what's up? You're in a mood!"

"I just want to be on my own."

"You haven't had another row with Sandy?"

"Elly, just leave it!"

"Don't bite my head off."

She was having trouble keeping up with him. His strides were long and she sensed the tension in his rigid arms. She took another chip, then tossed the remains in a nearby bin.

"I thought you weren't going to meet her. You said earlier that you hadn't arranged to see her."

They had just passed the turning for their road. Carl was heading for the sea front. He was going to the Beachcomber. Elise felt her mood lift. She could go there and comfort him.

"She was getting a lift home from her mum. That's what she said. Then I go and she's there with Fenner. The both of them sitting closely in the bus shelter. Cosy. Any chance he gets he's in there."

"Oh," Elise said, putting her arm on his, trying to slow him down, "it might be my fault again. . ."

He turned on to the sea wall ahead of her. She followed quickly. The cold air was slapping at them. Elise pulled her coat tight, her hands thrust down into her pockets. Carl's jacket flew open but he didn't seem to notice.

"I asked her to speak to him!" she called.

She pictured the two of them on the funny half seats of the bus shelter. Maybe Sandy was talking quietly into Peter's ear again, like at the party.

"Why is it always to do with you, Elly?" Carl said, raising his voice against the sound of the sea. "Every time there's any trouble you pop up. You're always there!"

She felt her jaw stiffen. They were almost at the Beachcomber. Carl had the keys out of his pocket.

"I don't get what you mean. I'm around because we're mates. We live next door to each. . ."

"Whenever there's a row you're there. You're with Sandy. You're with Peter! You're giving your opinion!"

"Only because you ask me. . . Sandy asked me. . ."

"I don't want to hear it!"

They stood facing each other. The Beachcomber was centimetres away. They could go inside, put the fire on, get warmed up. But Carl stood completely still. The sea was roaring and under it she could hear a knocking sound. It was coming from the Beachcomber; the wind riffling the wooden shutters.

"I'm just being honest!"

"You're in my face all the time!" he said, his voice scratchy. "You, Fenner. Fenner, you."

Elise felt her throat burn. "I don't want to see you get hurt..."

"Just leave me to sort my own problems!"

"It's not my fault if you can't trust your own girlfriend!"

"Who says I can't trust her?"

"You! You're saying it! No one else. Just you!"

He turned suddenly, towards the Beachcomber. He drew his arm back and punched the wooden door with his fist. Elise stepped back, shocked. Carl let his hand drop. Then he cradled it with his other hand.

"You've hurt yourself!" she said, incredulous.

"Go away, Elly," he said, quietly.

The wind was loud but she heard the words, each one cutting into her. She turned and walked away, her head down.

TWENTY-TWO

She stood in her room, her back rigid against the door. From downstairs she could hear the television playing, canned laugher and the loud voice of some actor. The house was hot, too hot for her. She felt herself sweating, her blood pumping round, firing her up. Her throat was raw. She was angry, incensed. How could Carl say such things? Tell her to go away! Say that she was always in his face. How could he? She kicked her school bag to one side and stepped across to her desk. Every bit of the surface was covered up: books, papers, photocopies, handouts. There wasn't a single space. How was she supposed to do anything in this mess? She put her hand out and swept it all to the side, sending a lot of it on to the carpet.

She looked round with dismay. The room was a mess. In any case it was too small for her. The whole house felt too small for her. She turned and walked out into the hall and straight into Andy's room. It was cooler there, everything neat and orderly. She sat down on the floor by the wardrobe. After a few minutes she pulled out the blue box and took out the cards and the photograph. In her head she could still hear Carl's words. *Go away, Elly*, he'd said to her. She, who was his closest friend. She, who loved him more than anyone. *You're always in my face!* Then he'd punched the door. Why? Who was he hitting out at? Sandy? Peter Fenner? Or her? No, no. He would never do that.

She opened a birthday card and read the words inside.

Why did she keep looking at these things? Over and over again. Was she trying to understand something, to fathom out the meaning of those few handwritten words in each of the cards, like some complicated code that she would crack? What did it mean? That her father had loved Andy and not loved her. What did it matter? He had still deserted them, still driven out of Colby East and not come back.

She thought of Carl, then, in the back of the silver car, chauffeured by Sandy's mum. One day, next June, he would be sitting in that car being driven out of the town towards the airport, going to Connecticut. There never would be any company. Carl and Elise; *M and H Renovations* was just what it had always been, a stupid daydream.

She put the cards back in Andy's blue box, neatly, among his personal things. Before replacing the lid, she wondered if Andy had other things from their father that he had kept safe. Letters, photographs, gifts even. The last card had come when he was twelve. There may well have been more. She had a powerful urge to see these imagined things, to hold them in her hands, to read any further messages Eddie Hanson may have left for his son. She stood up and looked around his room, her eye settling on the wardrobe, the cupboard, the desk, the chest of drawers, the bed. She felt her hands moving, itching to search, to do something.

She had to be methodical. She'd already been through the blue box. She looked keenly round the room. Maybe there were things among the mass of memorabilia that was on display. She went close up to the colourful badges attached to Andy's pinboard. There must have been thirty or more. An American Marine Corps shirt was pinned up on the wall and beside it the stars and stripes, overlapped by the Union Jack. On the shelves was book after book of military campaigns and wars. Would there be letters from Eddie Hanson in there, sandwiched in between the pages of a book?

She opened the top drawer of Andy's chest. It was full of things he'd bought on the web or at car boot sales. She picked up what looked like a brooch. It was shaped like the wings of some great silver bird. On the top, instead of a bird's head and beak, was a crown.

What was she looking for? A watch with an inscription, *To Andy, love Dad*? Or maybe a note that had been attached to a piece of memorabilia, a badge or a cap. *I found this on eBay. It was pricey but I know you like this stuff, love Dad.*

There were ties rolled up, showing old-fashioned aeroplanes embroidered on them. There were two caps, one newish, the other dark green, hard to the touch. It was old, she could tell, probably from the Second World War. It was one of Andy's prized possessions. As was his

Royal Marine Zippo lighter. Could either of those be gifts from Eddie Hanson? Andy was always bringing the lighter out to show people.

She rummaged round but there were no notes. She looked in some other drawers, making sure she left the clothes tidy before shutting them. At Andy's desk she looked in the top and side drawers but there was just stationery and folders full of leaflets and adverts for cars.

She opened the fitted cupboard in the alcove. In front of her was shelf after shelf of Andy's childhood things. She felt her spirits rise. His toys. Of course. Her father had left when Andy was eight. It was most likely that he'd buy toys for his son. And Andy had kept these; why would he do that if they weren't important to him? Who keeps their childhood toys? She certainly hadn't. Just as her eye was travelling up and down the books, boxed games, figures and electronic gadgets, she remembered something. Andy's secret hiding place. That's where he would keep something important, something precious; a gift from a father who was long gone. It was at the bottom of the cupboard, underneath the toys. She took them out, one by one. Boxes from a model railway set, battered but with edges taped up. A couple of Lego Star Wars sets, again, taped up. When she cleared the area she saw the light-coloured floorboards, the cut across the middle where they lifted up and showed a cavity underneath.

She allowed herself a wry smile. Andy never knew that she had found this place. When she'd been about ten she'd seen him crouched down at it one day and then, when he went out, she investigated herself. The space was about the size of a phone book but went deep, into the cavity between the floors of the house. The first time she'd looked at it she'd been startled to find two glossy magazines full of naked women. She'd sat glued to them for ages, appalled at the pictures, page after page of body parts. The next time she'd looked they were gone, but she found other things: a brand-new mobile phone still in its box, a couple of rolls of money and a flick knife. As time went on these things, mysterious in themselves, ceased to have any interest for Elise and she forgot about them. Then one day, much later, she looked and found it completely empty.

Now she pulled up the floorboards and leant into the cupboard to look down into the darkness. She could see a shape there, and when she put her hand down and pulled it up, she saw a red tin box. It had Arabic script on it, moving from right to left. Underneath were drawn pictures of biscuits or sweets, she wasn't sure which. Was it from Iraq? Was this where Andy kept his most secret things? She imagined a letter that had an address on it, an invitation to come and stay at Eddie Hanson's new home. *Dear Andy, Come and meet my new wife. She's tall and thin and has blonde hair. You'd like her...*

She edged the top of the tin off. Inside there were a couple of objects and she felt immediately deflated. One was wrapped in a wad of bubble wrap. She picked it up. It had a shape, something hard and curved at the centre. She knew she should put it back but she held it in her hand. It wasn't so heavy and yet it was solid. Then she noticed something else in the box, something covered in brown paper that had the word *cartridge* scrawled across it in black felt tip.

She wondered if it was a camera of some sort. A digital camera. Maybe it had photos on its memory card. Intrigued, she got up, went across to Andy's desk, got a pair of scissors out and started to snip through the tape on the bubble wrap. When it was free she began to unwind it, slowly, keeping the wrap in one piece for when she would put it back. When the bubble wrap was almost off she moved across to the bed and let the object drop on to the duvet.

She stared at it. It was a gun.

She looked again at the red tin box. She noticed some rust around the side and line after line of tiny Arabic script. The word *cartridge* resonated. A cartridge for a gun. Ammunition? She didn't know. She knew nothing about guns. Andy did, from his days in the army. That was always one of the first things friends and relatives asked him. *Will you carry a gun?* She remembered Andy being on leave and walking down the main road with him when Todd Bell pulled up beside them. He'd put one arm across the window of the car and shaped his other hand like a gun, his two fingers making the barrel. He'd made shooting noises as they passed and Andy had told him to get lost and grow up. Then, later, she'd seen the two of them standing outside the pub drinking pints.

Andy loved weapons. He had some in his collection of

memorabilia. He had had a couple of replica rifles once but had sold them on. They'd had solid barrels, she remembered, like sticks of rock without the writing. She turned and looked at the Swiss bayonet that was hanging on the wall, its blade sharpened and polished. None of this had ever held any interest for her.

She reached out to pick up the gun. She used her fingers like tongs and held it in the air. Was it a replica? She turned it round and stared up the barrel. It was hollow, like tubing. She dropped it back on the bed. She looked at the side of it. The words *Hackberry Armory USA* were on it in raised letters. It looked real. It was squat and its nozzle pointed like an angry finger.

She didn't like it being there.

She paced up and down for a moment. Had Andy bought it from some website? She glanced down at the red tin box, the Arabic script. Had he got it while he was in Iraq? Did he intend to sell it again? Was that what he had turned into? Some kind of small arms dealer?

It was dangerous. She didn't know whether or not it was actually loaded. It wasn't like a gun from one of the cowboy films, with loose bullets that had to be slotted in. It had an oblong handle that held a cartridge full of bullets. When it was empty it could be ejected and another put in its place. Was that what was in the brown-paper packet? Another cartridge?

She didn't like it one bit. A gun in the house. A gun that Andy had hidden somewhere. She picked up the bubble wrap and decided to cover it up again when she heard some movement from outside, her mum's footsteps on the stairs. She stood very still and listened. The bathroom door opened. Her mum was probably going to the toilet. She might not go straight back downstairs. She might pop into Elise's room and see what she was doing.

She was all fingers and thumbs but she put the gun back into the tin box and stuffed the bubble wrap around it. From downstairs there was a roar of laughter from the telly. She turned to the cupboard and shoved the boxes of toys back in. She picked the box up and went out of the room, closing Andy's door quietly behind her. She could hear the toilet flush and the sink tap running. She sat on her own bed, the tin box tucked behind her pillow. She heard her mum calling and then her room door opened.

"All right, Elly? You seemed a bit upset earlier. . ."

Her mum was looking round her room. Elise followed her gaze and saw her books and papers scattered on the floor.

"What's happened here?" her mum said. "It looks like a tornado's hit it."

"I'm having a sort-out," Elise said.

Her mum made a face and went out.

Elise grabbed the tin box and put it in a drawer underneath her jumpers. Then she got up and began to tidy her room, her mind buzzing.

A gun. Not a present from her father to Andy.

She lay down on her bed, her eye on the drawer. It was only a piece of shaped metal, an inanimate thing, and yet its very presence was making her feel uncomfortable. She turned on her other side. She closed her eyes and tried to think of other things. Carl, Sandy, Peter, Andy. Goodness knows she had enough stuff on her mind. But every now and again she remembered it there, in the drawer, aimed at the middle of her back.

TWENTY-THREE

She woke early. As soon as she opened her eyes she knew that the gun couldn't stay in the house. She hadn't slept well at all and over the course of the night, in her head, the gun had metamorphosed into something else. Instead of being a weapon that somebody needed to pick up and shoot, it now seemed more like a hand grenade, capable of going off by itself.

It was still dark but she got out of bed and pulled on some clothes. She took the tin box out of her drawer and handled it carefully, as though it held something breakable. She listened at her mum's door and heard the sounds of her regular breathing. Downstairs she put her coat on. She picked up the spare garage key and went out of the kitchen door and into the garden. The air was thick with cold, the ground crisp with frost. She was taken aback to see light coming from under the door of the garage. She put her key in the door and opened it slowly. Carl was there. He turned round instantly. She wanted to smile but instead she tensed, reminded of the horrible row they had had the previous evening.

"What's up?" she said.

It was just past six. She looked round and saw that the

heater was on and there was the muted sound of music coming from a radio.

"I couldn't sleep so I thought I'd do a bit of work. What are you doing in here?" he said, his eyes dropping to the tin box she was holding.

He looked rough, tired, his shirt done up on the wrong buttons. She glanced at his hand, the one he had used to punch the door. She couldn't tell if it had been bruised or injured.

"What's in the box?" he said.

The box. She looked down at it. She had thought to hide it on her own. Now that Carl was here she didn't know what to do.

"Just something of Andy's," she said, coldly.

"Elly, look, I'm sorry I went off the deep end last night. You caught me at a bad moment."

She shrugged and moved past him, round the jeep, towards the old cupboard where Andy stored odds and ends from cars he'd worked on.

"She was with Fenner at the bus stop. I'm sick of him always hanging around. I feel like punching his face. When you came along I just, I guess I just took it out on you."

She stayed quiet. She placed the tin on top of the cupboard. Carl had moved and was standing beside her. She didn't look at him.

"Don't give me a bad time about it, Elly. Come on, you're my mate. Tell me what I should do. Be my agony aunt," he said.

He touched her arm. His hand was warm and it made her skin rise. She felt a ripple of yearning across her chest. She didn't dare to turn to him, just stared at his hand. The knuckles were scraped; the skin was purple. She tutted and touched the sore part with her fingers.

"You've hurt yourself," she said, softly.

"I'm an idiot," he said.

They were close, centimetres apart. She could feel his shoulder next to her head and she wanted to turn round and bury her face in his chest. Hadn't she done that? On the night when he'd lay on top of her, kissing her neck and her hair until she was dizzy.

"What am I going to do? About Sandy and Fenner?" he said, stepping back towards the jeep.

"I told you last night," she said, clearing her throat, "I asked Sandy to speak to Peter, so I feel like it's my fault. . ."

"How come she does it with such fervour?"

"Fervour?" Elise said, surprised at the word.

"You know, close up, touching his arm. Every time I see her with him, she's like this much away from him," he said, holding his fingers out to make a point. "Like he's hard of hearing and she has to get close."

"That's the sort of person she is. She stands close. She's touchy-feely. She's American. They do things differently."

"I don't know. Life was easier before. When it was just you and me, down at the Beachcomber."

She was surprised. She had to hold her expression firm, to stop herself from crying out with delight. It was true. Things were better before. Even he could see that now.

194

"What's in the box?"

She turned to the tin box. It suddenly seemed alien to her. As if she'd never seen it before. The Arabic script looked like a secret code, the box an odd shade of red. It ought to have held something exotic. Instead it held an American gun. Why not show it to Carl? She'd always shared news of Andy with him.

"I found it in Andy's room," she said. "He asked me to look for something and this was hidden away."

He raised his eyebrows and came closer. She pulled the lid off and grabbed at the bubble wrap, pulling it out until the gun was visible. There, among the tools and mechanical odds and ends, it didn't look as ugly as it had the previous night.

"Wow!" he said, in a half whisper. "I've never *seen* a gun before."

"Neither have I," she said.

"Is it a replica?"

"I don't think so. Its barrel is hollow."

"Is it loaded?"

"I don't know. I don't think Andy would leave a loaded gun around. Here, in this envelope, there's a cartridge. That's how it's loaded, I guess. It slots into the handle."

Carl had the gun in one hand. Elise pulled the brown paper off the cartridge and held it out. It was the shape of the handle, black and metal.

"It's already got a cartridge in, I think," he said, lifting the gun up and looking at the base of the handle.

"I don't feel right about it being in the house. I thought

I'd put it in Andy's cupboard, and when he gets out of prison, he can get rid of it."

Carl was moving the gun from hand to hand, feeling its shape, turning it upside down. Eventually he placed it back into the tin box.

"It must be from Iraq," she said, turning over the lid of the tin box so that the Arabic script could be seen.

"Probably got it from an American soldier. He told me he spent a lot of time with them. They were always bartering stuff. He said that he had a few valuable things hidden away."

"He told you that? How come he never told me?"

"It's a bloke thing."

She didn't answer. She took the gun out and placed it on the bubble wrap and began to wind it around, like a bandage.

"I should go," Carl said.

"You won't tell anyone about this?" she said. "Not anyone?"

"You mean not Sandy. I won't be telling her. I'm probably going to finish it. I don't need the hassle."

"Really?" she said.

"Yeah. I mean, it was great, at first, but it's not so much fun now."

"Don't rush into anything."

"I just don't get why she has to be so friendly with Fenner."

"She's matchmaking. You wouldn't understand. It's a girl thing."

"Thanks," he said, lifting his arm and putting it round her shoulder, pulling her towards him in a rough hug.

Then he turned the music off and picked up his radio and went out the front of the garage. She heard the key turning in the lock. She stood stock still, hardly breathing. He was going to give Sandy up. It was going to be the way it was before. Would he do it? She wondered. She looked down and was momentarily startled by the red tin and the gun lying among the rucked-up bubble wrap. She pulled herself out of her reverie and began to gather it up and twist it back around, tucking it neatly back into the tin and pushing the lid on firmly. Then she squatted down, opened the cupboard and placed it on the bottom shelf among the tins of oil and metallic paint. Standing up, she scrutinized it. It fitted in with all other stuff in there. She closed the door. She found herself feeling lighter, happier. The gun was out of the house. And she and Carl were friends again.

Back indoors she picked up her mobile and looked at the screen. There was a message that she hadn't noticed the previous evening.

Give me a ring. We can meet up. Peter.

Sandy had done her matchmaking. She had got Elise's message through to Peter. She pressed the delete button. Why should she want to meet up with him when Carl was going to be free again?

TWENTY-FOUR

The dress rehearsal for the Christmas concert was on the last Tuesday of term. Even though Elise wasn't part of it she still got dragged into helping set up the hall. The performers had been given the afternoon off and the place seemed empty, save for the younger years stacking chairs and rushing round with notes in their hands for the music teacher, the drama teacher, the heads of year.

Carl had finished with Sandy. There'd been no great emotional explosion, no broken hearts, no crying in the girls' toilets. It had just happened and she had seen Sandy moving from class to class, sitting in the common room, walking towards her mum's car, practising her violin at lunch time.

What had she expected?

The world hadn't changed its axis. It hadn't been headline news. Carl and Sandy were no more. It had finished as quietly as it started. *I feel like it was my fault*, Elise had said, sitting beside Sandy in history. Sandy had waved away her apology. *It was absolutely nothing to do with you*, she said, smiling at Peter Fenner across the other side of the room.

For the past couple of days Elise had been busy in

Palmer's doing extra hours. She was helping to decorate the shop and change some of the produce around, Mr Palmer said, *to position the Christmas items to their best advantage, dear.* She had volunteered to do these things, deliberately keeping Carl at a distance. After the row she didn't want to be around him too much. She wanted to give him some space.

In any case, she'd had other things on her mind.

Every time she went out of her house or came back in she looked at the garage doors and thought about the gun. The previous evening she'd gone in and looked in the cupboard where she'd hidden it. Opening the door, she shifted some of the things about so that the red tin was behind a box of sandpaper. Then she moved a tin of varnish beside it. She was sure that no one would know what it was. No one.

Then there was her father. Her search of Andy's room hadn't produced any more things from Eddie Hanson. A couple of times that week she'd thought of asking her mum about him. *Why did my father contact Andy and not me?* She couldn't imagine doing it, though. Her mum wouldn't know what to say. She'd shrug and say, *Oh, I don't know.* She was wishy-washy. She didn't have opinions or strong feelings. She worried about things so that a conversation with her turned into a list of anxieties. If only Gran were still alive. Gran had been easy to talk to. She would be able to explain her father's actions. Gran knew their family history stretching back generations.

She'd taken the cards out of their hiding place yet again

and looked at them. She'd studied her father's handwriting, small and slanted. She looked at the picture, the denim jacket and white boots. Fashions from a different time. *To my lovely boy, Andrew. Love Dad.* She read it over, aware of a growing resentment in her chest. It sat there heavy and still, like a thunderous cloud. Dad. It wasn't a word that had any significance in her life. Up to now she hadn't cared one way or another. Edward Hanson was her biological father. His absence hadn't affected her. They had their family: Gran, Andy, Mum and Elise. They hadn't needed him. He was just a name on a bit of paper. Her father. But to Andy he had been *Dad*. The difference between the two words wasn't just in the spelling. *Father* was formal, distant; a tall man in a suit, standing away from her, untouchable. *Dad* was homely. She saw a man in denim sitting on a chair with a small boy on his lap, his hand curved around the child's back, his other hand holding a book open while he read a story.

Curiously, though, she no longer felt angry about it. Her thoughts strayed too quickly for her to build up any rage. She'd think of Carl and the hug he gave her. Sandy was in the past. She had everything to look forward to. She had no reason to dwell on things that had happened seventeen years before.

When school finished on Friday she hung around the common room, watching as various sixth-formers drifted in and out in their concert costumes. The choir were milling around, boys and girls in white shirts and dark trousers holding music scores. Sandy wandered in among others, looking distracted. She was wearing a long blue dress and matching shoes, like a bridesmaid. She held her violin and bow in the same hand, hanging low. Elise gave her a sympathetic smile. Then, without warning, the common room emptied, and some minutes later she heard the distant sound of warm-up music. The rehearsal had started. It was time to go home. Just as she was sorting through her locker, Carl came in. He looked round in a jokey way.

"They all gone?" he said.

She nodded.

"Going home?"

"Yes."

"I'll come with you."

They walked in silence for a while, leaving the sound of the rehearsal behind. It was bitterly cold and Elise zipped her jacket up to her neck and shoved her hands deep into her pockets. She could see Carl's breath in the air as they passed through the half-empty car park and out of the school gates. The road was busy, cars shooting by every few moments. They didn't speak but Elise was comfortable with the quiet. They walked along, their shoulders bent against the cold. They passed Marsh Park and Elise glanced in. The darkness was thick and heavy and she felt a blast of cold from the open ground. It made the tops of her ears sore. From nearby, somewhere, she could hear the bark of a dog.

Eventually she had to ask.

"You broke it off with Sandy," she said.

"Yep," he said crisply.

They'd come to the lane that led into town. She walked on the inside next to the hedge and he was at the edge of the pavement. Her shoulder kept hitting his arm, and when a car came he moved in front so that they walked in single file.

"Dad's picking me up in a couple of hours and I'll be at his place over Christmas. We've got that job to do. I told you about it. Then on Boxing Day we're going to West Ham. After that I'm coming home."

"Boxing Day. That's nearly two weeks."

"A week and a half. I need the break. And the money. What you doing?"

"Extra shifts in Palmer's. No one wants to work over Christmas and I can make a bit of cash."

"Christmas day?"

"No. Even Mr Palmer shuts then. I'm working Christmas Eve and Boxing Day and the day after that."

"Seeing Andy?"

She shook her head. "Mum's going a couple of days before Christmas. I'll do Mum's shift in the shop. I'm going to see him in January before his appeal."

She could see the lights of the town up ahead, giving the dark sky a honeyed glow. Looking round, in some of the outlying houses, there were the colourful lights of Christmas trees. It made her feel *festive*.

"You think Sandy will end up with Fenner?" Carl suddenly said.

"I don't know."

He began to tell her about going to his dad's and the job they were going to do in time for Christmas. Elise nodded and looked interested but really she was thinking about Sandy and Peter Fenner. Elise had never really considered the two of them *actually* getting together, not seriously.

"It was never about race," he suddenly said. "I don't think Sandy cared one way or another."

The comment threw her and she couldn't answer. She knew it was the truth. Two cars edged past each other on the lane and Carl went ahead of her. She looked at his broad shoulders and his hair cut tight into his neck and for a second she felt ashamed. How could she have hinted at it, made Carl think for a second that it was true?

"Look!" Carl said, as they turned into the town. "It's really Christmas. It's starting to snow."

On the last day of term everyone was talking about the concert. *You were great. No! You were great! We got the biggest clap! No, you did!* Working in Palmer's meant that Elise hadn't actually seen it so she avoided the chatter and the congratulations and excitement. When the final bell rang she got her coursework and revision handouts from her locker. She waited until the noise of the younger kids had all but gone and then left the common room.

The corridors had cleared and the whole place seemed deserted. She could hear her own footsteps echoing along. She passed the assembly hall, glancing in briefly. She went on for a few steps until she registered the fact that she'd seen a head of white hair through the glass panes in the doors. She stopped and reversed back and looked through. A few metres away was Sandy. Next to her was Peter Fenner, his droopy hair flicking round his face, his leather coat hanging almost down to the floor.

He leant down for a moment and kissed Sandy on the cheek. Sandy backed off but was smiling and talking animatedly.

Something lit up inside her. Maybe Peter and Sandy would get together. She stepped away from the doors, a smile growing on her face. Then everything would drop into place. She would have Carl and Sandy would have Peter. Turning a corner she almost ran into Miss Peacock, who was walking along with a couple of other teachers.

"Hello, Elise. You look pleased with yourself."

She was. She couldn't help it.

"Have a good Christmas, miss," she said.

"Merry Christmas to you too."

"And a happy new year."

TWENTY-FIVE

Palmer's was busy on Boxing Day. Elise started work at ten. She sat at the till while a variety of people shuffled through. They bought newspapers and boxes of eggs and batteries. They chatted in the aisles as though they hadn't seen each other for weeks. "Have you got bacon?" a woman asked briskly as she popped a dummy in the mouth of a small child on her hip. Elise pointed to the back of the shop where the refrigerators were. Children burst in and studied the sweets section, eventually coming forward with a handful of bubble gum, chocolate bars and sherbets. Teenagers from school wandered in. They looked tired and bored, eyed the cigarettes, but just bought packs of gum and mints.

The shop felt cold when she first arrived so she put the fan heater on and stood in front of it as hot air circulated round her legs. She looked around. The decorations which had seemed bright and dazzling now looked gaudy and tired.

Mr Palmer was in the shop for most of the morning. He was wearing a light-coloured jumper that Elise hadn't seen before. It was mauve and had different-coloured diamond shapes on the front.

"Rosemary's present for me. She got it from mail order, on the Internet. Not that I really approve of that kind of shopping but when you're disabled. . ."

"It's very nice," Elise said.

Elise thought about her own Christmas presents, the black trousers and blouse that she had chosen in the shopping centre in Norwich. *Always black these days, Elly, how come?* her mum had said, paying for them at the counter. Then there were the new high-heeled shoes that made her look and feel taller and thinner. She was wearing them round the house for short periods in order to get used to them. The rest of the time they sat neatly in the box, toes pointed forward. They were for special occasions. She intended to wear them to Jason Bell's New Year's Eve party.

Mr Palmer brought her a mug of tea just after eleven.

"You'll be all right on your own, Elise?" he said. "I have to pop out for a while but Maureen's due in at twelve so it won't be for long."

She nodded, glad to be on her own. She watched him go out into the street. He had a black plastic bag tucked under his arm and his eyes were blinking at the daylight. When he was out of sight she sat down at the till, angling the fan heater at her feet. The street outside was largely empty; most of the customers had come in cars, pulling up on the double yellow lines with no fear of parking tickets.

She wondered what Carl was doing.

She'd sent several light-hearted texts to him over the

last week. He'd replied with a line or two saying something about the job or his dad or something about Christmas. As each day went by she began to be more optimistic about the future. She got her coursework done and helped her mum prepare for Christmas, putting a pink tinsel tree up in the living room and dusting off last year's lights. She wrapped her presents for Andy and saw her mum off on the bus for the prison visit. She did a couple of night-time shifts in Palmer's for Maureen, who was unwell. When she got paid on Christmas Eve, she was surprised to see how much she had earned. Getting home, she took the notes up to her room and put them in her drawer. Tucking the money away, her fingers felt the silk vest. She pulled it out. The sight of it gave her an unpleasant feeling. Why on earth had she taken it? It was like a small dark cloud amid her good spirits. She folded it and folded it until it was a tiny oblong shape and shoved it in the back of the drawer.

She'd had lots of cards from kids at school, and on Christmas Eve she got a text from Peter Fenner: *Have a happy Xmas Elly!* She'd answered, *You too!* She'd wondered if he and Sandy had been seeing each other during the holidays. Living in the same village meant that they probably would. Maybe the peck on the cheek she'd seen on the last day of school had developed into something else.

The shop door opened and Jason Bell came in. She stood away from the heater and gave him a tiny smile. He had something in his hand, a small package wrapped in Christmas paper.

"Hi!" he said, sheepishly. "I thought you might be working."

He put the package on the counter. She frowned.

"It's for you."

She looked at it with surprise. A present from Jason? She'd hardly spoken to him in weeks. The last time was when she'd broken an arrangement to go round his house.

"Open it," he said, prodding it towards her.

He looked nice. His hair was longer and his skin was glowing, as if he'd walked all the way along the sea wall and back. She picked up the package. It was a small box, about the size of a CD, but it didn't feel like one. She stuck her nail in the edge of the paper and pulled it apart, peeling it off until she had a plain green cardboard box in her hand.

"You shouldn't have bought this," she said, gently prising the lid off. "I haven't got anything for you."

"It doesn't matter."

In the box was a necklace. It was a silver hoop with a heart-shaped pendant hanging from it.

"I can't take this," she said. "It must have cost a lot."

"No, it didn't. I want you to have it. Wear it to my party."

"Well, thanks," she said, leaning forward to give him a kiss on the cheek.

When he eventually left the shop, she felt ill at ease. The green box sat awkwardly on the counter and there was a squirmy feeling in her stomach. Jason had romantic ideas about her. If only things were clear with Carl. Then she could be straight with Jason once and for all. She patted her pockets, looking for her mobile. She would give Carl a call. She'd say, *On your way back? Fancy coming round my house?* She walked into the back of the shop and felt in her coat pockets. Her mobile wasn't there. She must have left it at home. She went back to the front of the shop and served a number of customers and then tidied the papers and magazines. All the while she was thinking about the call she wanted to make. Not having her mobile had made her mood plummet. The call, which was only for a bit of light-hearted chatter, became more pressing as the minutes ticked by. When Maureen came in for her shift at just after twelve she was straining to get out, to go home and pick up her mobile.

"I won't be long," she said. "Ten minutes at the most."

She followed the older woman towards the back of the shop and picked up her coat. As she was walking out she heard the sound of her humming and the tap running, water splashing into the kettle.

She was home in minutes. She opened the front door and slipped into the warm hallway. There were no lights on downstairs, no sign of life. She looked at her watch. It was twenty past twelve; surely her mum wasn't still asleep? As she walked upstairs she heard the muffled sound of a radio from her mum's room. Her mum was awake at least. She opened her mouth to speak but then stopped. She wasn't in the mood for any kind of conversation. She just wanted to pick up her mobile and get back to work. She went into her room and looked around. She saw it on the chest of drawers and picked it up. Halfway down the stairs she heard her mum's room door open, the music from the radio spilling into the hallway. She sighed. She couldn't just go without saying a word. She turned to go back up.

"Mum, I left my mobile. . ."

She stopped. There, on the landing, was Mr Palmer. He was standing still, doing his shirt up, his socks sticking out beneath his trousers. Over one arm was the mauve jumper that his wife, Rosemary, had bought on the Internet.

"Elly!" her mum said.

Her mum came out of the bedroom, walking around Mr Palmer. She had a silk dressing gown on that Elise hadn't seen before. It was pale pink and belted tightly at the waist, holding in her mum's breasts. Her long hair was hanging in strands over her shoulder.

"What's he doing here?" Elise said, her eyes travelling up and down Mr Palmer, taking in every detail: his beige socks, the trousers that looked like they were part of a suit, the pink shirt that he was struggling to tuck into his waistband.

"Why aren't you at work?" her mum said.

"I forgot my phone."

"Who's minding the shop?" Mr Palmer said.

She couldn't speak. She couldn't think of a single word. She stared at Mr Palmer's white skin and his dyed black hair.

"Elly," her mum said, reaching out to her.

She turned away and walked back down the stairs. From the landing she could hear their voices, whispering, as though they were hiding and trying not to be found, when it was too late; she had already discovered them. Mr Palmer and her mum. It was almost laughable.

She went into the living room, slamming the door. She sat on the edge of the sofa, her legs clamped together, her elbows on her knees. In front of her, on the wall above the mantlepiece, sat Gran's photograph. A glamorous young woman dancing in the chorus at Great Yarmouth. Her arms were crossed at the waist, showing long white gloves that went up to her elbow. On her head was a diamond tiara. Many years later it had ended up in Elise's dressing-up box.

With love, Marilyn. How beautiful she had been.

There was the sound of footsteps coming down the stairs. The door opened and there was a soft cough.

"Elise, dear. I hope there's not going to be any bad feeling here. I'm very fond of your mother..."

Mr Palmer's voice was tentative. Elise stared straight ahead at the photos. She wasn't going to answer him. Gran would have laughed out loud at Mr Palmer and his papery skin and his special telephone and his wife that no one had seen for months. Gran would have roared. *Oh, Sal, couldn't you have managed anything better than that?* she would have said.

"I understand, Elise. You're feeling a bit off-colour. Why don't you take the rest of the day off? We'll manage in the shop, don't you worry. And you won't lose a penny in wages."

She felt the door swing shut. She heard Mr Palmer calling goodbye to her mum. Then the front door banged and there were softer footsteps coming down. She closed her eyes. Her mum came into the living room. She walked across and stood with her back to the mantle, blocking the photographs. Elise was forced to look at her.

"You don't need to stare at me like that," her mum said.

"Like what?"

"As if I'm some kind of . . . loose woman!"

Elise spluttered out a laugh. Her mum was worried about *morals*. She was worried about bad taste.

"I like Billy Palmer. His wife's been ill for over ten years. She hasn't set foot out of that flat for the last two years. He has no life."

His name was *Billy*. Elise hadn't known that. It didn't fit. Billy seemed like a young person's name. Not Mr Palmer, who lived for his shop, who had skin like a corpse.

"You don't have to explain it to me. What you do is up to you. I just think you could have got someone better!"

"Is that what you think," her mum said, softly, moving to the armchair. She sat down with a sigh. She was still wearing the pink dressing gown. It had fallen open at the front and her dimply knees were poking through.

"He's just so . . . gross!" Elise said.

"Everyone has different tastes, Elly. I don't find him gross."

"Your taste in men is awful. First my father and now him!"

"Your father? What do know about him? You've never even seen him."

"I've seen a picture of him. I've seen what he looked like. In any case, it's not just about looks! Palmer's got a wife! He's abandoning her. What sort of man is that?"

"He's not abandoning her. He's looking after her. He'll never leave her. He's a good man. So what if he comes round here for. . ."

"A shag?" Elise said.

"A bit of company," her mum said.

"My father abandoned us."

"That's true. I can't deny that."

"Except for Andy."

Her mum frowned.

"Or maybe he kept contact with you as well. Maybe it was just me he cut out of his life."

"I don't know what you're talking about!"

"Wait here, I want to show you something."

Elise ran upstairs. She came back down with the birthday cards and the photo. She held them out. Her mum tried to take one but Elise shoved them all at her, spilling them over her lap.

"Cards sent to Andy on his birthday, for five years, and a photo – look, stuff written on the back. All for Andy."

"Where did you get these? Did Andy keep them?"

There was silence while she read through each one. Elise watched her eyes tracing the words on the pages.

"I can't believe he kept these. When I gave them to him he never said a word. Not a word. I assumed he'd chucked them away."

"You're missing the point!" Elise said, snatching the cards back, holding them out. "It's not that Andy kept them. It's that he had them at all. What sort of a father leaves his family and just keeps contact with one of his kids? What sort of man does that!"

Her mum stared at her. She had no answer. Elise began to pull at the cards, trying to tear them. But it was too hard, the wad was too thick. She threw them on to the floor and kicked at them.

"Don't. They're Andy's cards," her mum said.

Elly plucked the photo from her mum and tore it in half and half again, letting the pieces float down to the floor.

"Your taste in men is rubbish, but then I suppose you've got to take what you can get," she said, her arms trembling, looking at the mess on the floor.

Her mum's eyes glazed over. She blinked out a tear. Then another.

"You were a baby. Your father hardly saw you," she said, wiping her cheeks with the pink silk sleeve.

"What happened?"

"Things weren't good between us. Then you were born and he left soon after. It was like the final straw for him. Not *you* as such, just having another baby," her mum said, dropping down on to the floor, picking up the cards that Elly had thrown. She placed them on the mantle.

"Why did he keep in touch with Andy?"

"He'd lived with Andy for seven years. Me and Gran, we thought that it was all right for Andy to get the cards. We didn't think he cared about them one way or another. With you it wasn't so bad. You never knew your dad so you never missed him. Like your Gran said, *What you never had you never missed.* Me and Gran, we thought that of all of us, you were the lucky one."

The lucky one. Elise was the lucky one.

They were standing facing each other. Her mum hesitated for a moment, then took a step and put her arms around her. Elise could feel the slippery silk of the pink dressing gown. After a stiff moment she lifted one of her hands up and gave her mum a pat on the back.

"You were the lucky one, Elly," her mum's muffled voice came. "You never had your heart broken."

Elise closed her eyes. How little her mum knew.

TWENTY-SIX

In the afternoon, after her mum went to work, she tried to relax. She took a long bath. She listened to music. She watched television. She had no idea what time to expect Carl. The football match finished mid-afternoon, and then there was the journey from East London. She calculated that he might get there about five. After six she began to get agitated. She went to the fridge and saw the remains of a bottle of wine in the door. She filled up a stemmed glass and went upstairs to her mum's room. Leaving the light off, she stood by the window looking out on to the street.

She was desperate for him to arrive.

She drank the wine, tasting the cold sweet liquid. She looked out at the night sky. It was bright; she could see the stars. That meant it would be cold. She pulled a chair over and sat in the bay, looking down, waiting for the headlights of Michael's car to turn into the road. When she finished the wine she went downstairs and refilled her glass.

At seven she was pacing up and down the living room. There had been no call, no message. She didn't know what to do. Should she call him? Send a text? Wait? Or just go next door and ask for him? Isn't that what she would have done months before? When they were just mates?

She went up to her room and had a quick look in the mirror. She straightened her top and brushed down her jeans. She glanced across at the shoebox in the corner. Her new shoes stared back at her. Why not put them on? She picked them out of the box. She slipped her feet into the high heels, fastening the strap across the middle of her foot. Her varnished toenails looked bright against the black leather. She stood up, feeling as though she was on tiptoes. She walked to the mirror. She liked what she saw.

Moments later she closed the front door behind her. The cold air clung to her, getting in between her toes and up her sleeves. She hugged herself as she walked up Carl's pathway and rang the bell. She held herself tall and waited for someone to answer the door. If Penny answered she'd say, *Is Carl in?* If Carl answered she'd smile and say, *Hi, stranger!*

No one answered.

She pressed the bell again. She listened as it rang shrilly through the house. The hallway light was on but she couldn't see any movement. She looked at the bay window. The Christmas-tree lights were flashing on and off. She rang the bell a third time. From behind the glass she could see a door opening and movement. A shape came along the hallway. It was Penny. The door opened and she could see Penny's hair sticking up on one side, as if she'd just woken up.

"Hi!" she said. "Is Carl in?"

Penny sighed. "You've missed him. He's gone round to Sandy's."

"Sandy's? I thought they'd split up?"

"They made it up. Before Christmas, I think. You know what they're like. On one minute, off the next. Her parents have rented a cottage up in Wells. He's gone up there. He'll be back early New Year's Eve."

"I didn't know."

Elise felt the cold creep under her top, prickling her skin.

"You could give him a call?"

"I will," Elise said, backing up the pathway, the heels of her shoes grazing the ground. "I'll call him."

She went upstairs silently. She closed the door of her room and walked up and down, five, six times. When she came to a stop she found herself trembling, her hands in fists. How could he go back to Sandy? How could he? She sat on her bed and kicked off the shoes without undoing the strap. She was indignant, affronted, insulted. It wearied her. She felt like she'd been angry all day. All week. All year.

She'd waited the whole ten days for Carl. And all the time he'd been making it up with Sandy. *From before Christmas.*

She felt sick. She stood up and went towards the door, her hand up to her face. She could taste the wine, sweet and warm in her mouth. Was she going to throw up? She held on to the door handle trying to be calm, making herself breathe more slowly. After a few moments she stepped across to her chest of drawers and pulled the top one open. She picked out the silk vest. It was cold and it slid against her fingers. She put it up to her face, feeling her breath going in and coming out. A scent of something hit her. Was it the silk? The lace? Some distant perfume of Sandy's that had impregnated the fabric? She held it away, looking at its delicate straps and lace trim. Then she sat on the bed, heavy with loss.

How had it happened? Had Sandy rung him? Pleaded with him? Had she agreed never to speak to Peter Fenner again? Maybe she had actually gone to Norwich to see him. No doubt her mum, *the chauffeur*, took her in the silver car. She'd knocked on Michael's door and stood all pouty-faced, her white hair sticking out awkwardly, evidence of her heartbreak. *Oh, Carl, let's make up!* she'd say and press herself into him, sliding her arms around his middle. She'd wave to her mum in the car and say she wanted to stay a while and her mum would drive off, do some late-night shopping, while Carl took her by the hand and drew her up the stairs to the room where he slept in Michael's house. Elise had never seen that room. No, she had never been invited there.

Elise lay back on her duvet, the silk vest scrunched up in her hands. Her eyes were open but she wasn't seeing her room; she was seeing another room, somewhere in Norwich. Carl pulling Sandy across to a single bed, sitting down side by side. All the time Sandy would be talking but Elise had muted that sound; all she could hear was distant music, girls singing in harmony, a saxophone playing, and all she could see was Carl pulling Sandy's pale face to his and opening his mouth to kiss her. She saw it happen, watched as his mouth lingered over hers, his hand dropping down to the hem of her skirt.

It sent a surge of pain through her, a hot ache that filled her chest and throat.

She looked down and saw the silk vest up against her ribs. Taking a corner in each hand she began to tug and pull, only stopping when she heard the tear come, like a groan. She stared at it in her hands. Alongside one of the seams the fabric had split, its edges fraying. In spite of her anger she felt a sudden tearfulness. She'd messed it up. It was a beautiful silk and lace vest and she'd ruined it with her temper.

She would never have him. What had her mum said? *What you never had you never missed.* But it wasn't true. She would miss him every day of her life.

Her mouth seemed like it was full of saliva and she swallowed it back. She stood up, kicking her new shoes away from her. What did her life amount to? Overweight, too short, top-heavy; medium-brown hair, medium length, medium face. She was average. Nothing special. She would always be like that. She could buy shoes like her gran used to wear but she would never be anything like her. She was a girl who lived in a crap town on the east coast of England. She'd finish her schooling and work in a call centre or a shop or if she was really lucky she'd get a job in an office, an estate agent's or a building society. She'd end up like her mum, a couple of kids, errant husband, working in a shop. Maybe she'd even sleep with the boss. After all, who else would want her; just some creepy white-skinned man whose wife was too sick to go outside. The pattern of her life was in her genes just like the shape of her body. Small, fat, like her mum.

Not like Sandy. She would go back to the USA and have a glittering life. She'd stand on the white sand of a beach in New England. By the side of her would be Carl Murdoch, her prize from old England.

For a long while she lay perfectly still.

When she heard her mum coming home from work she sat up and forced herself to stop crying. She could sort this out. It wasn't over. She had put a stop to their relationship once and she would do it again. Sandy would not have Carl. She would not. There had to be a way to make Carl distrust Sandy. She would make it happen. This time once and for all. She picked up her mobile and scrolled through her call history. After a few moments she found the *Merry Christmas* message from Peter Fenner. She pressed the reply button and wrote the text.

Hope you had a good Xmas! I've got some probs with my Hist coursework. Any chance I can come round tomorrow? I wouldn't ask but I'm desperate!!!

She put the mobile down and waited for a reply. A

couple of moments later she heard the beep of his message.

Come and see me tomorrow afternoon about four. Looking forward to it. Peter.

TWENTY-SEVEN

Peter Fenner's house was the fourth along the street. Elise carried her rucksack low on her arm and walked up to the door. She rang the bell. It was just before four-twenty so she was a little late. A woman answered.

"Hello," she said, smiling. She was dark and thin with glasses on a chain round her neck. Before Elise could say anything she turned her head slightly and called, "Peter, your friend's here."

The hallway of Peter's house was almost as wide as her living room. On one side was a hall stand, groaning with coats. Standing out among them was the long leather coat that Peter always wore.

"Did you have a nice Christmas?" the woman, his mother, said.

"Yes, thanks."

Peter appeared and came down the stairs two at a time. His mother turned away and went off towards the back of the house.

"You got here all right?" he said.

He was wearing skinny black jeans and a T-shirt. He'd had his hair cut. It made him look more boyish.

"Bus took for ever," she said.

He hooked his thumb, indicating that she should follow him upstairs. She went up, thinking how easy it was to lie. The bus came right on time and sailed along, the roads virtually empty. The reason she was late was that it was somewhere she hadn't wanted to go. She'd dithered and messed around with her papers until the time for leaving had gone. In the end she'd forced herself out of the front door and through the town and on to the bus.

"In here," Peter said.

His bedroom was huge. Along one side were a number of musical instruments, drums and guitars on stands. Along another was a huge desk holding a computer and printer and games console, with two chairs at angles. The bed was in an alcove. The corner of the duvet was hanging on to the floor and the pillows were scattered. There were a couple of giant beanbags on the floor and several cushions. In the other alcove was a rail that held clothes. No wardrobe, just a chrome rail with hangers on it, like a dry cleaner's.

"Come in," he said. "Put your files and stuff here. We can look at the essay."

She gave a sigh. The finished essay was at home but she'd brought some notes and stuff so that it looked as though she hadn't started yet. She took her rucksack over to the big desk and unpacked it. Peter pulled up a chair and accessed a file on his computer. She took the other chair. She had her black cardigan on over a black stretchy sleeveless vest. It wasn't silky and had no lace and it hadn't been bought at a posh shop but it was tight and low at the front. She undid the cardigan and let it fall open. Peter's eyes flicked down and he seemed to shuffle in his chair a bit.

"I really appreciate your help with this," she said.

"No problem."

For ten minutes or so they talked about the work. Peter knew a lot about Cromwell and the Restoration so she wrote some notes. He suggested a plan and she jotted down bullet points. Apart from the mass of detail it wasn't that different to what she'd already done. When it looked as though they were nearing the end of the discussion, she decided to take it on a bit further.

"Did Sandy ever give you a message from me?"

He looked surprised. He nodded, his eyes moving away with embarrassment.

"I thought she was joking at first," he said. "I did eventually send you a text."

"By that time I wasn't sure. I had an idea that you and Sandy. . ."

She left the words hanging.

"Is that what Murdoch said?" he said, shaking his head.

"Maybe," she said. "I know Sandy has a soft spot for you and I thought. . ."

"Nah, we're just mates. We both like music – I mean, playing music."

"How's the band going?" she said, not wanting to push it.

They ended up sitting on the beanbags. Peter produced

some cans of beer and they drank while talking about his band and the boys he played with from St Benedict's. After a while he showed her their page on MySpace and told her about the CD they were putting together and how they were going to market it themselves. Elise was impressed. She'd only ever seen Peter as an odd lad. There was more to him, though.

"Are you on MySpace? Or Facebook?"

She shook her head.

"You should put up a page. It's a great way to network. Sandy's got a page on MySpace. I helped her do it last week. Do you want to see it?"

She nodded. He started tapping keys and the screen changed. It took a minute for the page to materialize. She thought about what he said. *It's a great way to network.* Why would she need something like that? She had never been someone who felt the need for loads of company. She had people to sit with in school, girls and lads to chat to from time to time. But she had always had Carl. Why would she have needed a big group of friends?

Sandy's image filled the screen. It was in black and white. The page was cut into sections: her eyes, one side of her face, her toothy smile, the back of her head, her white hair standing on end. There were chunks of text in between the pictures.

"Weird."

"I did them. I took my digital camera over to her place. Look at how white she looks. Her skin is like milk. It was difficult to photograph. Her hair kept merging into her face so I had to airbrush it so that it shone. I'm quite proud of it!"

Elise studied the page. Sandy's chalky face stared out at her. It was put together last week when Carl was away. Had Sandy told him about it? she wondered. Would he be happy that Peter had spent so much time at Sandy's house while he was away in Norwich?

"If you like, I could do a MySpace page for you. I could take some photos. You could write a blog. We could call it ellysweirdworld.com. It's really simple."

She was momentarily thrown. She looked at the screen and imagined herself there. Elly's weird world. She smiled. Was that possible? That she could have a page that people would look at and admire? She focused on each of the images on the screen. Sandy's eyes stared back at her. Her white hair looked almost silver, her teeth completely straight and white. What would her picture look like? Her brown hair hanging to her jaw. What was interesting about that? Just like a million other girls. Her MySpace page would be one that people quickly flicked over.

She must have looked unhappy because Peter took her silence to mean something different. He put his hand on her face and pulled her round so that she had to look at him.

"I'm not with Sandy. We really are just mates."

She nodded and he leaned forward and kissed her on the mouth. She responded, reaching up for his neck. The kiss sent a shudder through her. How long had it been since she'd been kissed? Weeks before. She opened her mouth and pushed her tongue against Peter's, her head feeling light and woozy.

"Wait," he said. "Let's sit down."

He meant the beanbags but she went across to the messy single bed and sat on it. When he joined her she shrugged her cardigan off and sat with just the vest on. Her neck felt cold but her chest was tingling, her skin electric. He ran his hands up and down her arms and then she lay back and he lay beside her, his fingers sliding the vest straps off her shoulders.

Peter's dad gave her a lift home. Like Peter's mother, he wore glasses, heavy black frames that he took off and put in a case before starting the car up. Elise and Peter sat in the back seat of the car and held hands. At her house he got out and walked her to her door, where he gave her a tiny kiss on the mouth.

"I'm out tomorrow. Come round on the day after. You can show me how far you've got with the essay."

"I'm at work," she said. "I could come round on Tuesday."

"See you then."

She nodded. When he left she stood on her door and watched the car drive away. In her room, later, she took her mobile off silent and looked in the inbox. There was nothing. No text from Carl, no unanswered calls.

Three days later she was in Peter's bedroom lying side by side with him on the single bed. She was hot, her skin on fire. Her blouse was undone and Peter was touching her, making her move around in a restless and frustrated way. He looked uncomfortable himself, as if he were on the brink of saying something, of doing something new, something *risky*. Instead, he sat up, buttoned his shirt up and climbed over her to get off the bed.

"There's some wine in the fridge," he said. "I'll get it."

"Won't your mum miss it?"

"She doesn't mind me drinking alcohol. In *moderation*."

When he went out she sat up and tidied herself. She straightened the duvet and plumped up the pillows so that they were a comfortable backrest. Then she leant against them and waited for Peter to return.

That morning she'd sent a text to Sandy.

Thanks for your help with P. Me and him are now together.

She pictured Sandy showing this text to Carl. *There, you see*, she'd say. *I said they were suited for each other. I told you there was nothing between me and Peter.* And what would Carl say? This thought made her feel uncomfortable. She had a lot of things in her head that she would have *liked* him to say. Maybe, in truth, she would have preferred him to nod and not reply at all. Then she could imagine that his feelings were mixed. Elly with Peter. He would be relieved that Peter was spoken for. But with Elly? Was that what he really wanted? Wasn't there, somewhere deep inside Carl, a tiny bud of regret that they had never got together?

The door opened and Peter came into the room holding

two stemmed glasses and a bottle of white wine that was almost full. He put them on to the desk and poured each one out. She took her glass and he sat himself down beside her. He began to talk about the new song his band was recording and she nodded but she wasn't really listening.

In her head she had an image of Carl looking at Sandy's text. He would nod and smile but it would only hold his interest for a second and then he would turn back to Sandy and feast his eyes on her. His golden girl.

Elise took a gulp of wine. It was cold and dry and she let it slide back down her throat.

"How many guitars do you own?" she said, looking round the room.

"A couple. The rest belong to the band."

"What about the violin? Who plays that?" she said, seeing a violin case leaning up against the wall.

"That's Sandy's. She left it here last week."

"Sandy was here? In your room?"

"There you go again. There's nothing between me and Sandy!"

"Why was she here?"

"We were playing around with some of my songs. She played violin in a couple. We might even ask her to come and play with us at St Benedict's."

"She never said. . ."

"No, we had to keep it hush hush. What with Murdoch being so edgy. But now – with you and me – it shouldn't be a problem."

Elise nodded and drank her wine. She kept drinking, her eye settling on the violin case. Sandy had been visiting Peter secretly for a while. She wondered what Carl would make of that. She put her glass down on the carpet and took Peter's glass away from him. Then she moved further down the bed, pulling his arm so that he came too. When he was facing her she kissed him lightly.

"I'm sure Carl will be fine about it," she said, reaching for his belt buckle and gently undoing it.

On the morning of New Year's Eve she was up earlier than she needed to be. She couldn't sleep. She was fidgety and irritable. She went in her mum's room and sat down on the side of the bed. Her mum was dressed, leaning close to the mirror to fix some earrings in. She was wearing red trousers that were too tight. On the floor was her overnight bag.

"What time are you due at work?" her mum said.

"Three to eight."

"You won't be rude to Billy, to Mr Palmer."

"I won't say anything to your boyfriend," she said, sighing heavily.

"You haven't forgotten I'm going to Jackie's."

She shook her head. Her Aunt Jackie, who lived in Ipswich, was having a party.

"The invitation was open to the both of us," her mum said. "It'll be a laugh."

"I told you, I don't want to go. There's no one my age there! Anyway, I've got Jason's party to go to."

"Don't bite my head off. I'll be off soon. I told Jackie I'd get there early and help her with the preparations. You will be all right on your own?"

"I will. I said I will," she said, her voice softer.

After her mum had gone Elly stood at her bedroom window and pulled the curtain back so that she could see out into the street. Penny had said that Carl would be back early. What did that mean? Nine o'clock? Ten o'clock? Or did she mean early afternoon?

She had no choice. She would have to wait and hope that he came back before she had to go to Palmer's.

At just after eleven the silver car pulled up outside and Carl got out, giving a wave as it drove off. On the ground was a bulging rucksack and he picked it up and walked down his path without so much as a glance at her house. She watched him and felt an ache across her ribs. She hadn't seen him for over two weeks. His hair had got longer and he looked fresh and bright, as though he'd spent every day in the fresh air walking along the beaches of north Norfolk. A few seconds later she heard his front door bang.

She waited.

An hour later she sent him a text.

Come round if you can. I've got something important to tell you. It's about Sandy and Peter.

Then she waited again.

TWENTY-EIGHT

There was a knock on the door a few minutes before she was due to leave for Palmer's. She opened it hurriedly. It was Carl. She'd given up expecting him to come. She'd been dejected all day long and here he was, smiling on her doorstep.

"All right?" he said. "I only just got your message. I can't stay long. Sandy's coming round soon."

She felt a stab of disappointment. He'd only been on his own for a few hours. Did he have to see her so soon? She glanced at her watch. She was going to be late for Palmer's but it didn't matter. She pulled the door back. He looked uncertain, as if he hadn't intended to come in. Then he walked past her and headed for the kitchen. He seemed so big, broader and taller than Peter. She noticed that he was wearing a jacket that she hadn't seen before.

"I hear you're with Fenner?" he said. "Glad that all worked out in the end."

He stood with his back against the unit, the jacket firmly zipped up. It was a fleeting visit, she could tell. He had no intention of spending any time with her.

"I hear that you're back with Sandy," she said, frostily. "That was a surprise."

He shrugged, a sheepish smile on his face. She studied the jacket. It was a dark-blue windcheater. There were no labels on it that she could see but it looked expensive. She wondered if it had been a Christmas present from his dad. Or Sandy.

"You said you had something to tell me? About Sandy and Peter?"

He was getting straight to the point. He was smiling but there was uneasiness behind his eyes. As if he didn't want to be there. She felt her confidence slipping away. It was better to get it over with before she lost her nerve.

"I think there is something going on between them. I'm sorry to have to tell you this, especially since you've got back together. . ."

He shook his head dismissively.

"I always thought you were imagining things when you went on about Peter and Sandy. I tried to calm it down, don't you remember? Here, in this room, when you were angry because Sandy had Peter's book?"

"It doesn't matter now, it's in the past," he said, shuffling his feet as if he was getting ready to go.

"And you asked me to be your agony aunt, remember?"

"That was a joke."

"I've liked Peter for a while," she said, rushing on, "and it was nice of Sandy to put a word in for me, but it didn't feel like it was the right time, so when everyone was away I called him and that's how we got together. I've been round his house a lot this week. I do like him but he never stops talking about her."

Carl didn't answer. His face had no expression. She carried on.

"When you were away they were together a lot. Believe me..."

"How do you mean, *a lot*?" he interrupted her. "I know they spend time together. They both play music. He lives near her. They were in the concert together!" he said, exasperation creeping into his voice. "It was you who said all these things to me in the first place. You who persuaded me to chill out!"

Chill out. One of Sandy's phrases.

"That was before I got to know him. Before he told me things..."

"What things?"

"He made her page on MySpace. He took photos of her. Did she tell you that?"

"She said he helped her..."

"He did it all! They spent ages on it. He talks about it all the time."

"So he helped her, so what. I knew that!"

"And she was in his bedroom helping him to practise his songs. Her violin is there among his guitars. She's been doing it for weeks. *Sandy's so good at the violin. I might ask her to join the band*, he said." She mimicked a soppy voice, a note of panic in her words. Was he believing her?

"She was in his bedroom?" he said.

She nodded. "Nearly every day, when you were in Norwich with your dad. Did she tell you that?"

He looked like he wanted to say something but didn't.

"Why would she keep it from you? If it was innocent?"

"How come Fenner's with you? If he's so keen on Sandy?"

"To try and make her jealous! I think he wants her to choose between you and him."

Carl's face had creased up.

"And I saw him kiss her, at the end of term, on the last afternoon. They were in the hall together. On their own. He kissed her on the cheek. Did she tell you that?"

Carl gave a tiny shake of his head.

"I'm sorry to have to tell you this," she said.

"Why do you want me to break up with her?"

"I don't! But I don't want you to get hurt either. And I'm annoyed about Peter. I've waited all this time and it turns out that he's using me to get someone else."

"He *kissed* her?"

Elise nodded.

"And she's been in his bedroom?"

"You ask her!"

"I will."

"And he kept talking about her white skin. *She's so white*, he said."

"White?" Carl said.

"That's what he said."

"Why'd you bring that up?"

"Because of what you said before Christmas when you'd finished with Sandy. You said you didn't think race was an issue with her. I was telling you what Peter was going on about. I don't know whether Sandy is worried about the fact that you're black."

"Mixed race."

Elise nodded. "I know. I meant that."

There was a beep from Carl's mobile. He got it out of his pocket and looked at it.

"Sandy's at my house," he said.

"What are you going to say to her?"

"I don't know," he said.

He walked out of the kitchen and a moment later she heard the door bang. Her heart was thumping. She looked at the time. She should have been at work twenty minutes before. What did it matter. Mr Palmer wasn't likely to tell her off.

About an hour later Sandy came into the shop. Elise was stacking cans of lager in the refrigerator. The shop door opened and she heard Sandy's voice. She knew it was her immediately. She walked out of the aisle and saw her standing at the till. She was wearing skinny jeans and a duffle coat. Her hair was flatter than usual, not quite as white. Elise waited to see what she had to say.

"Please don't tell Carl things about me that aren't true! You've got it wrong about Peter and me. We're friends. I thought you of all people knew that."

Elise shrugged. At the till Maureen was looking at Sandy, then at her, then back again.

"Just butt out!" Sandy said and turned and went out of the shop.

Butt out! Butt out! Another Americanism. It was the best Sandy could do. Elise didn't mind, she wasn't offended. Maybe now they really would split up. It couldn't happen soon enough.

TWENTY-NINE

She took her time getting ready for Jason Bell's party. She was alone in the house and so she put some music on. She left the bathroom and bedroom doors open so that she could hear the sound filling the upstairs. She moved gently to the thudding beat and the voices of girls singing in harmony. In the background a saxophone played silkily as she showered, washed her hair and dried herself. She hummed along with it, whispering the lyrics as she stood wrapped in a towel, drying her hair.

Tonight she wanted to look her best. She felt as if this party was some kind of turning point. She hoped Carl would be there and that he would stay with her for most of the evening. She doubted Sandy would go. Perhaps she and Peter would stay in Little Cumber, practising tunes on his guitar and her violin.

It was almost ten. She didn't want to be too late. She pulled on her black jeans and top. She fished out her new shoes and slipped her feet into them. She got her make-up bag out and took out a new red lipstick that she had bought. She leant towards the mirror and pursed her lips.

She stood back and looked at herself. The top was tight

against her chest but she didn't mind. The colour minimized her breasts. She liked the look. The slim fit of the jeans over her high heels made her legs look as though they went on for ever. *Legs like a dancer.*

The song was filling her head and she began to move from one side to the other; a slow dance, her shoulders and hips swaying. She noticed how her lips shone and her toenails stood out like tiny rubies. She closed her eyes and let her arms move up in front of her, her palms flat, her legs swaying in a liquid way.

A sound distracted her. It was underneath the music. She kept moving to the beat but the sound nagged at her for a few seconds until she realized that it was the doorbell. She stopped. She turned the music off and went downstairs, taking care not to knock or scuff her new shoes. She opened the door. Carl stood there. He looked dishevelled.

"Hi," she said. "You OK?"

He walked past her without a word. She closed the front door.

"I'm just getting ready to go to Jason's. Come upstairs."

She walked ahead of him, feeling a frisson of excitement that he was behind her, going up to her room. The landing was steamy from the long shower she'd taken. She closed the bathroom door and he went in ahead of her and sat on the bed. The room seemed harsh and bright. The bed was a mess of cast-off clothes. She turned the centre light off, leaving only the bedside lamp, which cast a pink glow around the room.

"Are you all right?" she said, picking up her bag and putting her mobile and her lipstick in it.

"Why did you say all that stuff about Sandy and Peter?" he said.

He seemed unsteady. Was he drunk? Stoned?

"It's what I think," she said.

"Sandy says it's not true."

"She didn't go round Peter's to play his songs? She didn't let him take the photos and do her MySpace page?"

"She did," he said, an edge to his voice, "but she said that was all it was."

"Why didn't she tell you about it, if it was so innocent?"

"Because she knew I'd get upset. She said she wanted to be honest but was worried that I'd go off the rails."

"And the kiss? What did she say about that?"

"It was a friendly kiss. A Christmas kiss."

She shrugged her shoulders.

"She says they're friends. She's always said that. Why would she lie to me? If she wanted to go with Fenner she'd just dump me. It's not like she's *married* to me."

She stood with her back against the chest of drawers. Although he was only a step away he seemed in a different place. She wanted to reach out her hand to touch him but felt she might hit an invisible wall.

"I don't know what to say. . ."

"I keep asking myself, Why would she lie?"

"Why should I lie?"

The bed was a complete mess. She leant forward and plucked up the clothes she had been wearing before her shower. Carl shuffled along, getting out of her way.

"I'm not saying you're lying. I'm just saying maybe you're reading it all wrong. Sandy has loads of friends. She's a friendly person. You're different."

"Are you saying I'm not a friendly person?"

"You're more. . ." He stopped for a moment. He looked confused. His reply came slowly. "You're more reserved, stand-offish. Everyone knows that. Elly keeps herself to herself."

His words were slurred: *hershelf to hershelf*. She felt herself becoming irritated. Was he saying she had no friends? That no one liked her? It was ridiculous. She was never short of people to talk to.

"Sandy's different. She draws people to her. She likes to be among lots of friends. In the States she has a big gang of friends, girls and guys. She collects them, she told me. She has a whole *collection* of friends."

In the *States*. Girls and *guys*. Sandy had taken over Carl's words.

"She's *touchy-feely*. You said that."

She didn't answer. She thought that this was all sorted but it looked like she still had to persuade him. She was suddenly tired of it all. She looked down and realized that she had her old clothes over her arms. She began to fold them. He moved along the bed to lean against the headboard, pulling the pillows up to cushion himself. It was an action that made her relax, to see how easy and comfortable he could be in her room.

"She's American. They do things differently. You said that."

"She might be American but he's not," she said, wearily.

She wasn't going to argue any more. She turned slightly and caught her reflection. The crown of her head was just scraping the top of the mirror. Amid her frustration she had a moment of pleasure like a single beam of sunlight breaking through a wall of cloud. She remembered Peter Fenner's words. *With some sunglasses you could look like a French film star.* Maybe she would buy some. Tomorrow, on New Year's Day. A new Elise. Even her name had a French sound to it, Peter had said.

She looked down on Carl as he rested on her bed. He looked a mess. She, on the other hand, looked better than she ever had.

And still he didn't want her.

"I've got to go out," she said, pulling herself out of the moment.

He let out a big sigh and pulled himself into a sitting position.

"We should try and be friends. You and Fenner. Me and Sandy. We should hang out together," he said, turning round to fix up Elise's bed, straightening the pillow and the edge of the crumpled duvet.

Hang out together. More of Sandy's words. She watched him with a feeling of resignation. She was never going to take him back from this girl. Never. For the next six months she was going to have to watch him and her together, in school, in town, next door. And it would only end when Sandy and her family went back to the States and took Carl with them. Then Colby East would be bleaker, colder, emptier than it ever had been before.

"What's this?"

His voice snapped her out of her thoughts.

He was holding the pink silk vest in his hands. She looked at it with surprise. Hadn't she put it away in the drawer?

"What is it?" he said. "It looks like something Sandy wears."

He leant across and held it under the pink lamp, looking at the straps and the front and running his fingers across the tear. Where had it been? Under her pillow? Crumpled up in her duvet?

"Is this yours?" he said. "Sandy has one, I think."

He was staring at the vest, moving the lace through his fingers, looking at the label.

"It's from Bloomingdale's. That's a shop in New York. That's where Sandy gets lots of her clothes. I don't get it. Is this yours?"

He held it out and stared at her, confusion on his face. She looked at it with mounting panic. What could she say? How could she explain it?

"It's not yours, is it? You don't buy things from Bloomingdale's?"

She looked away.

"It's too small for you! Is it Sandy's? How come you've got it?" he said, staring at her.

"I. . ."

What could she say?

"How come it's here, Elly?"

She turned away from him and tidied the top of her chest of drawers. Her thoughts were racing. Amid the turmoil there was a prick of pain. *It's too small for you.* Sandy's top was too tiny for Elise. How would she fit her gross body into Sandy's slippery clothes?

"This is definitely Sandy's."

This was worse. He *knew* it was her vest because he'd touched it in the past. He'd run his fingers over the fabric, let his hand rest on Sandy's tiny breast. Maybe he had even leaned down and kissed the skin at the top of her arm while sliding his fingers underneath the lace.

She felt sick at the thought.

"How come you've got it?"

His voice was louder because he'd stood up. She could feel him behind her, towering over her, waiting for her to spill out the truth: *I took it! I stole it! I tore it!*

She couldn't say that. She couldn't expose herself to him, to let him see all the bile that had been inside her over the last weeks. She pulled her thoughts together and turned back to him. She held out her hand and he reluctantly passed the vest to her, his face suspicious. It felt cold even though he'd been holding it. Her fingers ran up and down the tear that she had made. She put her hands on each side and pulled it wide. It was small. Petite.

Not for her. She felt his impatience, silent, like a train in the distance, moving towards her, bearing down on her. She spoke, slowly and precisely, her tongue like paper, her words dry.

"I didn't want to show you this. I wanted to keep this from you," she said, offering the top back to him. "It is Sandy's top and I found it under Peter Fenner's pillow. It's one of the reasons I've been so upset. I found it there a couple of days ago. I didn't want to show it to you because I knew it would upset you."

He didn't answer, just stared at her.

"He must have kept it as a momento. I took it... I probably shouldn't have, but..."

Carl turned away and sat back on the bed. He looked winded, as though someone had punched him in the stomach. She sat down beside him, tucking her feet one behind the other, the heels of her shoes brushing against the end of the bedclothes. She put her hand on his arm. It felt limp.

"I can imagine how it happened. Maybe one day, when you were away, she was round there, playing her violin, laughing and joking with him. Maybe they kissed. Maybe they were sitting on his bed and one thing led to another. I know how easy it is. I've been there. I've sat on that bed."

He was staring ahead, the vest in his hands.

"Perhaps he asked her to take off her top," Elise reached across and took the top from Carl's fingers, pulling the tear apart. "Maybe he tried to help her. Maybe he couldn't wait and he pulled it and it tore..."

Carl stood up.

"Maybe Sandy likes to collect boyfriends," she went on. "She has you – her *black* boyfriend – maybe she also wants a white one as well."

He spun round to her. She moved back, fearful. He looked like he was going to punch out again. Like that night at the Beachcomber. Instead he snatched the vest from her hands and walked out of her room. She heard his footsteps down the stairs and then the front door slammed.

The house was quiet. Too quiet. She pressed the play button on her stereo and turned the sound loud so that the room was flooded with music.

PART THREE

THIRTY

New Year's Day
Morning

Peter Fenner was dead. Lying on the tarmac in Marsh Park.

Elise crept away like a ghost. A whey-faced girl with her hands in her pockets drifting about the town. She was disoriented, turning this way and that, heading first for home, then changing her mind and walking back towards the shops. After a while she slumped into a bus shelter, hugging herself, and watched the rain slanting down, hitting the windscreens of parked cars. Everything was dripping wet: the road, the pavements, the glass sides of the shelter. She looked down at herself. Her leather jacket was glistening. She wiped her hand across it and saw a smear of water. Her jeans were soaked, a tide mark riding up them. She felt her hair. It was hanging in strings. How long had she been standing in the park? An hour?

She'd gone straight there after Carl's call. It came at 6.27. She'd only been in a kind of half-sleep and her ring tone had sounded mournful in the blackness of her bedroom. She reached for it immediately. He could hardly speak. His voice was scratchy, husky. "I've done it, Elly," he said. "I've done a terrible thing. In the park." A few moments later the call was cut. She got dressed quickly and ran downstairs. She put her coat on and picked up her keys, intending to go straight there, find Carl and see what had happened. She went out of the front door and was about to go along the street when she saw the garage light on. She looked closer. The doors were closed but the cracks in the wood showed the light from inside.

A dreadful feeling took hold of her. She walked up the drive and pulled the door towards her. *No*, she kept thinking. *No, no, no no.* She put the light on and edged her way round the jeep to the cupboard that held Andy's tools. The door was hanging open. Some of its contents were lying on the ground. She saw the lid of the red tin box. Further away, upside down, was the bottom. She upended it. It was empty, the bubble wrap lying among the mess, like a membrane that had been discarded.

The gun was gone. She felt her stomach turn inside out.

She ran through the dark streets, only pausing for breath. When she got to Marsh Park she stopped, afraid to go in. She stood by the gate.

It was the first day of a new year and she watched as the darkness faded before her eyes and the swings and the slide and the metal horse emerged from the shadows. The body was at the edge of her vision and at first she couldn't bring herself to look at it. It lay out of sight as she stared at the soft rutted ground under the swings. Then she turned her neck to look and felt her breath freeze in her throat.

I've done it, Elly, I followed him to the park and now he's dead. That's what Carl had said. Her eyes clung to the shape on the ground. The rain fell on him and the wind pulled at the end of his leather coat, making it flap. She wanted to go across and do something. She really did. She even took a step but her body would not let her. Instead she backed away, circling the play area until she felt the ground change under her feet. The tarmac became soft grass and she turned and ran across the playing field to the trees so that she could hide herself away from him. She couldn't leave, though. She had to stay there and wait and watch. And all the time she knew one thing for absolute sure.

This was her fault.

Once the ambulance came there was nothing else for her to do.

A van passed the bus shelter. The windows were steamed up so she couldn't see into it. She followed it with her eye until it disappeared, heading for the road that led out of the town. She wondered if it would pass police cars coming from other places, speeding along the country lanes to get to Marsh Park, to find the person responsible. Her hand was wet and trembling with cold as she pulled her mobile out of her pocket and pressed the call button. It went straight through to answerphone. *Hi! It's Carl. Leave a message.*

She was startled by his cheery voice in her ear.

"Ring me. I can help you," she said, her voice cracking with emotion. "Ring me as soon as you can."

She started to walk. Where was Carl? Where had he gone? The rain pattered on her jacket. There was no one around, not one other person. The houses that she passed were closed up, their windows sealed with thick curtains, their front doors shut against her. After a few minutes she got to the sea wall, leant against the railings and held her face up for the sea wind to chaff. In front of her the sea swung from side to side, slurpy and brown, the gusts of rain pitting it.

She turned towards home.

Around her the town was coloured in different shades of grey. The rain had turned to a fine mist, so slight she couldn't see it hitting the ground. As she walked along she saw tiny signs of movement around the place. People were waking up to New Year's Day. A front door opened and someone came out in a padded coat with the hood up. They walked off, their heels making a scraping noise in the empty street. A car door slammed somewhere and a dog barked frantically on and on.

Further down the high street, outside Palmer's, a BMW pulled up. It was Todd Bell's car. She paused and watched with some vague hope that Carl might emerge but it was only Sue Perkins who got out. The car pulled away from the pavement the second she shut the door, its revs loud and brazen. Elise turned away and walked home. Nearing the house she saw, with dismay, that the garage door was still open. In her rush she'd forgotten to shut it. She went inside. The light was still on. She went round the jeep to the driver's door. The sight of the red tin box lying empty made her stomach contract.

Her fault, her fault. It was all her fault.

She shivered. It was cold in the garage and she was wet. She got into the driver's seat. Her clothes felt damp, her feet soggy. She hugged herself, looking away from the mess of things on the garage floor. After a few moments she got her mobile out and called Carl again. *Hi! It's Carl. Leave a message!* She did it again and a third time. Each time she waited to hear his voice, chirpy, upbeat. A recording he made months ago. A voice from the past. How different to the hoarse, cracked words he had used when he spoke to her that morning. *I've done it, Elly, I followed him to the park and now he's dead.*

Where was he? Was he shivering out in the cold somewhere?

She sat there for a long time. The light was on and the garage was bright yellow, as if there was too much light for such a small space. She looked around at the old jeep, its dashboard flat and grey, showing only a couple of dials, its steering wheel thin and plastic, grooves where the fingers should rest. There was no glass, just plastic sheeting over the windscreen. She glanced at the rearview mirror and saw two eyes looking back at her.

Her own reflection.

She looked closer, tilting her chin. Her lips looked pale and dry and her eyes were heavy. She looked palid and ill. How different to the night before when she was glossy and sparkling, when everything had seemed possible.

Her mobile sounded. The words *Carl Calling* were on the screen. She answered the call with a whisper, her hands trembling from the cold.

"Elly," he said.

"Where are you?" she said, her voice low, looking around the tiny garage as if there might be someone hiding, listening to her call.

"Elly, I don't know what to do! I don't know where to go!"

He was crying. His voice was loud and then low, as if he was moving around, changing direction, losing the signal then getting it back again.

"Did you see him? In the park?"

"Yes, yes, I saw him."

There was silence. It was deep like a black hole.

"Carl, come round to my house," she said, gently.

She climbed out of the jeep, pushing lightly on her leg, which seemed to have gone to sleep. There was no answer from Carl.

"My mum's not here. She won't be back from her sister's till this afternoon. Come round. We can work something out!"

"We can't. It's too late, it's too late. . ."

"Come round. We can talk about it."

"No amount of talking's going to sort this out."

"Meet me somewhere. I've got money. I can help you."

"At the Beachcomber. I can get there in twenty minutes."

The call went dead. She walked up and down, pins and needles shooting through her leg. Carl needed her. She had to keep her head. She owed it to him.

THIRTY-ONE

Halfway to the Beachcomber she saw a police car. The sight of it shook her but it slid past without a sound. It was headed away from the sea, out of the town. She didn't let herself visualize where it was going. She hurried on. She knew that the Beachcomber would be locked so she'd have to wait behind one of the beach huts until Carl turned up. She turned on to the sea wall and walked quickly. The sea was splashing against the groynes, sloppy brown waves see-sawing up against the wood, the seagulls springing off when the water got too close. Nearing the Beachcomber she saw that the door was at a funny angle, and when she got closer, she realized that it was hanging open a few centimetres. The padlock was on one side, dangling by its hook. She took it off. She pulled the door open and saw that the light was on and so was the fire. She glanced around to make sure no one was behind her and then she stepped inside, pulled the door closed, and put the latch on.

The place was a mess. On the floor was an old coat of Carl's, amid empty cans and smoking paraphernalia: papers, filters, scraps of tobacco, an empty plastic bag. A half bottle of vodka was on the worktop. This was Carl's stuff. Had he come straight here after leaving her house? Before the shooting? When everyone was at the party? When the bells were counting down to twelve and everyone was standing round, looking at the clock, waiting for the moment when the new year started?

She tidied it up. She put the cans and smoking stuff on the worktop and picked up the coat. Underneath she saw the pink silk vest. The sight of it shook her. She knew Carl had taken it with him when he left her house but she hadn't expected to see it. She picked it up and shoved it in her pocket, taking her mobile out at the same time.

It was almost eight. He would arrive any minute. She leant against the counter. After a few moments her thoughts went back to the party at Jason's the night before.

She arrived just after ten-thirty. She hadn't expected to see Sandy but when she went into the kitchen to get a drink she was there. Beside her, as bold as brass, was Peter Fenner. They didn't say a word to her, just eyed each other as she got a drink for herself. She didn't care. She turned to walk out of the room and there was Jason.

"You haven't worn my Christmas present!" he said, giving her a quick hug.

"It didn't suit what I was wearing," she lied.

She'd forgotten all about the necklace with the silver heart. She must have tucked it away in a drawer somewhere. He led her through into the living room, where coloured lights flashed on and off and the music was loud. She took a gulp of her drink and was startled when he turned and kissed her lightly on the mouth.

She backed away, making a joke of it. She half-expected Carl to show up looking for Sandy or Peter. She didn't want him to see her with anyone else. She wanted to be there for him if there was an argument or a fight.

The door opened and Todd Bell appeared, pulling Sue Perkins behind him. Without saying a word Jason went across to his brother and dropped easily into conversation with him.

Sandy and Peter came in and started to dance together in the middle of the flashing lights. Elise watched as Sandy moved her thin body one way and then the other, fluttering about, her white hair catching the coloured lights, looking like some exotic parrot that had landed among the pigeons.

Peter caught her eye and held it coldly for a moment.

Elise left the music and lights and went upstairs to the bathroom. She looked in the mirror and reapplied her lipstick, taking care to get it right. She was about to go out when she heard Sandy and Peter coming up the stairs talking. She stood and waited.

"I just don't want anyone to see me crying," Sandy said.

"That's all right, just go in the room where the coats are. Everyone else is downstairs."

Elise heard a door shutting and she went out on to the landing. Jason's room door was closed. She could hear

Sandy sniffing and crying from inside and Peter's soothing voice.

She got her mobile out and composed a text for Carl.

I'm at Jason's party. I've just seen Peter and Sandy go into Jason's bedroom and close the door. It's up to you if you believe it or not! Elly.

It wasn't as if she was telling a lie.

Elise was pacing up and down, waiting for Carl. The boards of the Beachcomber were groaning and creaking beneath her.

Where was Sandy? At home, in bed, sleeping it off? Oblivious to what had happened? She pictured her bedroom, all that old furniture, her silk duvet cover and the tiny sequinned cushions that crowded up her headboard. There was the old hall stand with her clothes hanging from it. Tasteful. Arty. Rich. She would be sleeping soundly, unaware of what had happened in her name.

Her mobile rang. It was Carl. At last.

"Where are you?" she said.

"I can't get there. Don't wait for me. Just go home!"

"I'll meet you somewhere else. . ."

The line went dead. She tried to call him back but all she got was his voicemail: *Hi! It's Carl. Leave a message.* She tried again and again. With her thumb she pressed the call button and listened over and over to his voice.

A knocking broke into her thoughts. It was hard and loud and it startled her. She pulled the latch back. The door swung out on to the beach. Penny Murdoch was there. She looked surprised to see Elise. She walked past her into the café.

"Where's Carl?" she said.

"I don't know."

"He rang me. He left a message. He was upset, crying. What's happened? Has something happened to him?"

She looked at the stuff on the side, the vodka bottle, the plastic bag, the filters and tobacco.

"He's into drugs? That's it, isn't it? He's taking drugs!"

Elise didn't say yes or no. Penny would find out soon enough.

On the walk back from the Beachcomber Penny strode ahead of her. She was puffed up with indignation, no doubt preparing some kind of lecture for Carl, maybe even a trip over to Norwich to see Michael so that they could all deal with the drug problem as a family.

But it wasn't drugs.

Penny reached home first. She stood by her front gate until Elise got there.

"Would you do me a favour? Would you ring Carl's friends, see where he is?"

"They'll be asleep," Elise said, hurriedly.

"I don't mean now, *this minute*. I mean this morning. I need to find Carl, see what sort of mess he's got himself into."

She gave her a look of reproach, as if she wanted to blame her. Then she softened, her shoulders dropping.

"Oh, Elly, this is not your fault. I'm just angry at Carl.

This is my worst nightmare. Single mum, son on drugs. It's just the worst..."

Elise nodded blankly, her feet carrying her towards her front door, her key out, pointed, waiting to slot in and get her inside the house.

The heat hit her. She stood for a moment with her back to the door and let the warm air drift over her. In her pocket she felt the silk vest. She pulled it out and held it up to her face. It felt damp. It no longer had the distant smell of Sandy but was briny, as if the sea air had penetrated its fibres. She unzipped her jacket and slung it over the banister and went upstairs, rushing into her own room and lying sideways on the bed, her knees up, her face pushed into the duvet. She slid the vest under her pillow. The house was completely silent except for the click of the boiler and some gurgles as water moved through the radiators.

She thought of Marsh Park.

The detectives and pathologists would have come. They would have erected a tent over the body and the whole of Marsh Park would be taped off. Someone would search the dead boy's pockets and there would be something there, a cash card with a name on it. In seconds there would be an address and a visit to his parents. Mrs Fenner with her glasses on a chain round her neck. Mr Fenner sitting next to her on the settee. *Do you know where your son is?* the police would say, and alarm would register in their faces.

Once they knew the dead boy's identity it wouldn't be

hard to find out about the party at Jason's house. She pictured the police going there, waking up Jason, demanding to know who had been at the party, where the firearm had come from, who had been after Peter Fenner. It would only take a second for someone to say that Carl Murdoch hated him.

Now she stood up and began to pace her bedroom. She had to do something. Phone calls. Penny had wanted her to make calls. She could do it, see what everyone else knew. She went downstairs to get her mobile from her pocket. The screen lit up. There was a message from Carl.

Don't look for me. I've got to see someone. I need to do it on my own.

She didn't know what to do. Why wouldn't he let her help him? She felt hot, sweaty, damp. She opened the front door to get some air. Parked outside her gate was a police car. The sight of it made her stomach rise. The car doors opened at exactly the same moment and two uniformed officers got out and walked towards Penny's front door. She stumbled backwards, into her house.

How long would it be before they told her? Minutes? Seconds? She couldn't listen. She had to get out. She pulled her coat on and looked at the message again. *I've got to see someone.* He must mean Sandy. Elise would go there. That's where she would find Carl.

THIRTY-TWO

After taking money from her drawer Elise walked straight to the minicab office. She paced up and down the tiny waiting area and made herself look at the cartoons on the small television that was perched on the wall. She overheard the woman on the radio talking to one of the drivers about a fight in Marsh Park. "I think there's been a stabbing," she said. A scratchy voice spoke back over the radio but Elise couldn't make out what was being said and the woman answered, "No, I can't, I'm off at twelve."

A police car went past and she watched it with a feeling of dread. It seemed to be moving in slow motion, the officer inside looking pointedly out of the window as it went by. She stopped pacing and forced herself to stand still.

The drive to Little Cumber was quick. The driver dropped her on the green. She paid him and waited until he drove off before she turned and looked down Peter Fenner's street. There, in front of his house, was a police car. It jolted her even though she'd half-expected it. She turned away and walked quickly back across the green and down the turning that led to Sandy's house. She looked at the time. It was ten past ten. It seemed like she'd been up for twenty-four hours. She stood in the lane and wondered what to do. The Christmas-tree lights were blinking on and off in the downstairs window but the blinds were drawn in the upstairs rooms. Were they still in bed? She got her mobile out and wondered whether to call Sandy. What would be the point, though? She was looking for Carl. If he was already in that house there was nothing she could do for him. She imagined him sitting on the silky duvet, his back against the sequinned cushions, telling Sandy what he had done. No doubt she would run for her parents and they would ring the police. *It's best to give yourself up*, Sandy's mother would say, her long white hair pulled back off her face with a black Alice band.

What could she do?

She looked at the side gate and noticed that it was open a few centimetres. She stepped towards it. The key was still in the lock. She pulled it out. It was old and rusted. She had one like it at home under a pot in the front garden in case anyone got locked out. She pushed against the gate and it swung inwards. She could see the wood of the gazebo at the end of Sandy's garden. She pulled the gate closed. She edged along to the corner of the house and listened hard. There wasn't a sound. Maybe all the occupants were still asleep. She walked out on to the wet grass a couple of steps, bracing herself for someone to shout out and say, *Hey! You there! Where do you think you're going!* She looked round. The conservatory was all shut up and the windows had blinds on them. She took a few more steps and was at the gazebo. She stepped on to the porch. All the windows had venetian blinds; it seemed as though everyone was hiding themselves away. She saw a gap where one of the slats had cracked and fallen. She put her hands on each side of her face to block out the light and looked through the glass.

There, lying on the sofa, his eyes closed, was Carl. Her breath caught in her throat. She'd found him.

She opened the door and went in, closing it quietly behind her. It was dark, just edges of daylight peeping round the blinds. She took a step and Carl moved, his eyes springing open.

"Sandy?" he said, in a loud whisper.

"It's Elly," she said.

He sat up. "What are you doing here?" he said, blinking up at her, rubbing his eyes with the backs of his hands.

"I want to help," she said, sitting down beside him, putting her hand on the back of his arm. His skin felt clammy.

"You can't," he said.

He lifted his hands up to his face and covered his eyes. She raised her arm as if to hug him but he was tight, closed against her. She touched his hair, her finger brushing against him like a feather, but he shrugged it off, edging away from her on the seat. She couldn't comfort him. Not after what he'd done. And all the time she knew something that no one else could know. *It was all her fault, every bit of it*. She sat still and composed but inside her throat felt fiery, as though there were a naked flame there.

"What happened?" she whispered.

He shook his head.

"I know you took the gun."

"It was an accident," he said.

She nodded, willing him to go on.

"I just wanted to threaten him. To frighten him. He's been in my face so much..."

"I..."

She started to speak, but what could she say?

"I'd been drinking, smoking dope." He was sitting forward, his elbows on his knees. "I thought I'd go to the party and give Fenner a pasting. But when I got your text... I was just going to smack him but then I remembered the gun."

She couldn't meet his eyes. Her text. Her words. It all came back to her. Anguished, she looked down. By his foot, on the floor, was the gun. The sight of it made her stomach crumple. She leant forward and picked it up, holding it gingerly. She expected it to feel warm, to burn her skin, but it was just a piece of metal and plastic.

"In the park it was so noisy. I kept shouting at him but he wouldn't turn round."

"He couldn't hear you," she said, miserably, "because of the fireworks."

Elise remembered the fireworks. The pops and bangs and whooshes that startled her and filled her ears. She was still at Jason's party. They were in the tiny back garden and she was holding a cup of wine and toasting the new year. Sandy had gone and she couldn't see Peter either.

Jason was inside somewhere, having a smoke. Todd Bell was standing next to Sue Perkins. Elise had been distracted by a peculiar red dress that Sue had on. When the clock struck twelve, the first fireworks started to go off, popping and fizzing, and Todd Bell pulled Sue Perkins towards him and started a long, deep kiss. Elise couldn't take her eyes off them until a rocket exploded in the sky and she looked up to see shards of gold shooting everywhere.

"I was just holding the gun, waiting for Fenner to turn round, and then it went off. It was like someone had punched me in the shoulder."

There was an image in her mind of Peter Fenner standing in the park. Could he have been looking up at the fireworks? Was it at that moment that the gun went off and his knees buckled and he fell on to the ground?

"I didn't mean it but no one will believe that," Carl said, wretchedly.

He turned his face away from her, moving his knees up, curling himself into a ball. She looked hopelessly around the gazebo. What was going to happen to him? What was he going to do?

She had to pull herself together.

"I'll get rid of this," she said, business-like, putting the gun into the pocket of her leather jacket. "You should leave. Go to Norwich. I've got money for you."

"I want to see Sandy," he said, "I have to explain."

"You're just wasting time. They're all asleep. It could be hours. . ."

But just then there was noise from outside. The door of the conservatory opened and there were voices. In the distance she could hear music from a radio. She went over to the venetian blinds and edged them apart. Sandy was there, in the conservatory, talking to someone who was out of sight.

"I'm going out to see her," Carl said, standing up.

Before she could speak he walked out of the door and across the grass. She followed him, her hand in her pocket, holding the gun. Sandy stood completely still when she saw him. Her face was first startled then annoyed.

"What are you doing here?" she said. "And why is *she* here?"

Carl started to say something and then stopped mid-sentence. He went rigid. When Elise saw what he was looking at she felt weak, her legs like rubber.

Peter Fenner was there, in the conservatory, standing next to Sandy.

"What?" Carl said, stepping back, looking shocked.

Sandy came out into the garden. Elise watched her walking towards them, a tiny bird of hope fluttering in her chest. Had there been some weird mistake? Was he not dead? Peter Fenner was standing there large as life.

"The most terrible thing happened," Sandy said, coming up to them, stopping a few paces away, making eye contact with Carl but ignoring Elise's presence. "Jason Bell's been *shot*. In Marsh Park. He's been lying there all night."

A choking sound came from Carl.

"Isn't it awful?" Sandy said.

Peter walked out into the garden. Elise's eyes clung to him. She could hardly believe it.

"How come there was a police car outside your house?" she said.

"Jason took my coat. He borrowed my coat."

"At first they thought it was *Peter* who was dead!" Sandy said.

"Jason might have been going to meet someone. To pick up drugs. He was shot in the back, the police said. Maybe he was cold. Maybe that's why he took my coat."

"This happens in the States but I never thought it would happen here."

"Do the police know who did it?" Elise said.

"Not yet," Peter said, his voice sounding heavy and unreal.

"Sandy, I. . ." Carl started.

Sandy's parents appeared in the conservatory, her mum in a long dressing gown. They looked puzzled.

"The police said that drug dealers often use that park," Peter said.

"I just don't know who could do such a thing," Sandy said.

Carl looked like he might speak but turned abruptly and walked away, towards the corner of the house.

"Is there a problem, dear?" Sandy's mother's voice rang out, silkily.

"Where's Carl going?" Sandy said.

Elise turned to follow him.

"What's happening? Why is Carl upset? Does he know something about poor Jason? Elly, what's going on?" Sandy shouted, her words cracking up.

"Leave her. You can't believe a thing she says. . ." Peter said.

She ignored the voices behind her and followed Carl out through the side door. He was running and had got to the top of the lane. She quickened her step even though she knew, in her heart, he didn't want her with him. When she got to the green he was further away, as if he'd sprinted. He was walking in the direction of Colby East. She thought she'd catch up with him further along, try again to persuade him to get away. She heard the sound of a car coming and stepped aside to let it pass. It was a van. Up ahead she saw Carl holding his arm out, his thumb up, hitching a lift.

The van pulled up a few metres on from him.

She watched him get in without a backwards glance in her direction. Then the van drove off.

She put her hands in her pockets. In the right one she could feel the gun. She let her fingers curl round it and walked on.

THIRTY-THREE

She had to walk from Little Cumber to Colby East. At first she went quickly, as if there might be some chance that she could catch up with Carl. After a while she slowed down. What was the point? Carl was in a car, miles ahead.

She put her hand in her pocket and felt the gun there. She stopped for a moment and looked at the hedgerow. She considered throwing the gun over into a field. Who would find it there? A farmer, maybe, but not for months, years even. Without the gun what evidence would there be? She pulled it out of her pocket. It lay on the flat of her hand, too big for her palm. It was just plastic and metal but it had taken a life. The words *Hackberry Armory USA* were stencilled on the side. How many other lives had it taken? In the past? In Iraq?

She thought of Andy in his prison cell completely unaware of what had happened. He had bought the gun from someone, an American soldier perhaps. He had hidden it away for some purpose of his own. To sell on? To add to his collection of memorablia?

Now the gun had memories of its own.

She shoved it back in her pocket. There was always a

possibility that some child playing in the field might pick it up and think it was a toy. She quickened her steps, wanting to get to town. The rain had completely dried up and it looked as though the sun might come out. She was feeling too warm. She unzipped her coat and took it off, letting it hang over her arms, making sure the gun was wedged against her stomach. She moved one foot after the other in a robotic way.

Jason Bell had borrowed Peter's leather coat. Jason Bell who had kissed her just hours before. Who'd bought her vodka and lemonade to drink in the back of his brother's car. A few days before he'd given her a Christmas present. A necklace. She hadn't even bothered to wear it. Now he was dead. She should have felt grief. On another day she might have. Today every flicker of feeling she had was with Carl. Jason was just a boy she had known. Carl was everything.

She got to the junction and looked both ways. In one direction was Norwich. Maybe the van Carl had got into was going that way and he'd decided to stay in it, to head for Michael's house, to tell his dad what had happened. On the other hand, it might have turned left towards the sea and Colby East. In which case he might have chosen to go home. What would he do if the police car was still parked outside his house? Run away, hide somewhere?

Just then she heard a car coming along the lane and moved on to the verge. It didn't pass, though; it slowed up and the horn tooted a couple of times. When she turned round she saw, with dismay, that it was the BMW and

Todd Bell was driving. Beside him was Sue Perkins. He sat there as if he was waiting for her to get in. Sue Perkins was speaking; she saw her lips moving and he nodded his head. It occurred to her for a horrible moment that he might not know about his brother, that he was on his way back from somewhere and hadn't been told. Had he and Sue Perkins pulled over to offer her a lift? How would she manage, sitting in the passenger seat? Would she have to be the one to tell him that his brother was dead?

Elise took a couple of steps towards the car and at that moment the driver's door opened and he got out and stood leaning on it. She knew then that he did know about Jason. His face looked red, blotchy, stricken. He stared coldly at her, biting his bottom lip, as if he blamed her for what had happened. She didn't move any closer to the car.

"I heard about poor Jason," she called.

The passenger door opened and Sue Perkins got out. She wasn't wearing the red dress any more. Of course not, she'd gone home and changed. Her face was still, her body language hushed.

"Where's Murdoch?" Todd Bell said.

"I . . . I don't know."

"You do know where he is. His girlfriend just told me he was with you. Where is he?"

"He got a lift," she said.

Todd Bell slammed the car door and walked towards her. His big face had dropped; his plump cheeks looked heavy. He was walking with both arms hanging like a sullen bear. She found herself stepping backwards. Her jacket was slipping over her arms and she couldn't go any further because the hedge was behind her. He came as close as he could, his big stomach poking at her, his chest in her face. Behind him she could hear Sue Perkins' voice.

"Give her a slap, Todd. No one would blame you."

"I know it was him, Elly. He was seen in Marsh Park with a gun. Don't try and deny it," he said, his hands grabbing the tops of her arms and squeezing them.

"I don't know, I really don't know," she said.

He was hurting her, his hands like clamps on her skin, and she began to struggle a bit.

"I'll hurt you, Elly, I'll really hurt you if you don't tell me where he is."

She couldn't move. She couldn't tell him anything. He was swearing and calling her names and saying stuff about Carl and she was trying to push him off. Sue Perkins had come over and was shouting at her and goading Todd on. Suddenly, without thinking, pulling strength from somewhere, she kneed him in the groin and he staggered back, on to the road, a look of fury on his face. He must have had hold of a bit of her jacket because he pulled the whole thing with him and it hung on his hands as he tried to defend himself against any further kick.

She had no intention of doing anything else and was about to turn and run, leaving her jacket in his hands, when there was a noise of something dropping on to the tarmac.

The three of them looked on to the ground.

The gun was there.

"It's not mine," she said, and she meant to go on and say that it was Andy's, that it was all a terrible mistake and that no one meant to for it to be used.

"I know. It's Murdoch's," Todd said, sharply.

"Murdoch's." Sue Perkins echoed his words.

He kicked her jacket out of the way, bent down and picked the gun off the ground. Without another word he pulled Sue Perkins' arm and walked back to his car. It only took seconds, not long enough for her to think. The engine rumbled and she felt the car rush past and heard it accelerating up the lane in the direction of Colby East. They would get there in minutes. She was a couple of miles away.

Elise pulled her mobile out of her jeans pocket. She pressed Carl's number. She expected the answerphone: *Hi! It's Carl. Leave a message!* She was going to tell him that Todd Bell was looking for him and that he had the gun.

But there was no answerphone. Just a flat noise indicating that his mobile was no longer in use. He'd run out of credit. The line was dead.

PART FOUR

THIRTY-FOUR

New Year's Day
Afternoon

There was a crowd of people on the sea wall. Elise was among them. She didn't stand at the front even though there were lots of kids that she knew there. She felt less visible where she was. She looked forward, avoiding eye contact with anyone. The tide was out and the beach stretched out before her, vast, brown and sodden. It was past twelve o'clock and the sun was sitting high in the sky. She shivered and pulled her coat around her.

Further along, lying on the mud, was Carl Murdoch. He was face down, his arms in front of him as though he'd tried to break his own fall. She knew it was him because people around her whispered his name in awe. *Carl Murdoch's been shot! It's Carl Murdoch! It's Carl. The Murdoch boy!*

A few metres away from him was an old motor boat, its hull resting on the seabed, its paint cracked and peeling, rust creeping up its sides. She could just pick out its name painted in italics, *Daisy May*. It didn't look as if it had moved for years.

The police were there. Some of them were holding back the crowd, others were walking out across the seabed to where the body was. They stepped carefully, as though they were afraid of sinking; or maybe they didn't want to get the bottoms of their trousers wet.

Elise stood on tiptoe and looked at the police car that was parked further up, alongside the Beachcomber. She could see the shape of Todd Bell standing by it, his arms out in front of him, as though he was leaning on the car. On each side of him was a policeman. A few metres away, talking to a WPC, was Sue Perkins. She was holding her hands up in a kind of protest, her head shaking from side to side.

New people were coming from the town. A silver car was parking further up. Its doors swung open all at the same moment and Sandy and her parents got out, as well as Peter Fenner. Sandy had a hand up to her eyes, shading the bright sunlight. Peter had a short jacket on, which he pulled tight to keep out the cold. He looked different. Elise was used to seeing him in his leather coat.

Did they know what had happened? As they got closer Elise saw that their faces were tense and sombre. Sandy's sunny expression had been washed away. Her mouth was pinched and her shoulders rounded.

There was no sign of Penny or Michael Murdoch. Elise's eyes scanned the crowds but neither of them were there.

She forced herself to look back out to sea, her eye resting for a moment on the line where the water turned into the sky. How far away was it? Twenty miles? Fifty miles? What would it be like to be there, in a boat, gliding through the flat sea, on her way somewhere?

Her eyes dropped back to the spot where Carl was lying beached on the mud. Something tightened in her chest. She took a gasping breath and felt grief filling her lungs, her stomach, her throat. She tried to move but it seemed as though her legs were made of wet sand. She leant against the person next to her and made herself listen to the voices around; like chattering gulls they told the story. It was a single shot in the middle of the boy's back. A revenge shooting for a drug deal that went wrong. It was something to do with Todd Bell's brother, Jason. No, no, someone else said. The boy's black. It was a race thing. She wanted to turn around and say, *No, he's not black, he's mixed race.* But it didn't matter. Nothing any of them said mattered.

He looked alone. She wished she could go to him, to cover him up, to sit by him.

There was a siren coming near. She wondered if it was an ambulance, maybe the same one that took the body from Marsh Park that morning, its blue light blinking on and off as it hurried down the lanes and into Colby East.

"Drugs," someone said, "the trouble they cause. Two boys shot dead in one day." People were talking around her and across her. She closed her eyes and looked down. Inside her head a voice was screaming out but no one could hear it. It was as if she wasn't there. No one could see her. She was invisible.